Seduction.com

Omegia Keeys

Passionate Writer Publishing
Indiana

Passionate Writer Publishing

www.passionatewriterpublishing.com

All characters in this book are fictitious, and any resemblance to real persons, living or dead, is purely coincidental.

ISBN 978-0-9843504-2-1

Manufactured in the United States of America.

First Edition

Dedication

This novel is dedicated to my loving and caring grandmother, Big Ma, you are the rock, foundation, and glue to our family. Without your love for all of us we would not be the strong, loving, caring, supportive, and hard working family that we are today. I thank you for raising a strong woman who could show me how to look past the madness and stay focused on my goals. I love you Big Ma!

Acknowledgments

I would like to acknowledge my family for keeping me grounded and for all the good times we have shared. My mother for never passing judgment and always pushing me, my oldest sister for praying for my soul as she reads this, all of my girlfriends who were supposed to help edit (I am still waiting), and everyone who supported *Passionate Playmates.* My high school English and Spanish teacher, you know who you are, thank you for starting that book club and taking interest in us young black girls. My close friends, we have come a long way but there is still a lot of road in front of us. Thank you all for the love, the laughs, and the tears. To anyone who has ever known me, yes I still have jokes. Laughter is good for the soul. To all the lovely ladies of Sigma Gamma Rho Sorority, Inc., keep on being the true essence of a Sigma Woman. And finally, if I forgot anyone I am apologizing in advance, but I am sure you will still let me know.

P.S. It's just fiction, so have an open mind. Now sit back, relax, and prepare for seduction.

Chapter 1

Erika pulled her black leather chair forward getting a better view of her girls in action. She looked at each of her models toying with their individual clients. Erika had 45 online employees and 15 were online at the moment. The models were made up of different sizes, shapes, and nationalities. She had a woman for every man's want and need. She watched on as Desire, a Latina goddess, put on a show pretending as if the man she was performing for was in the room with her. She was wearing a black sheer gown with a plunging neckline and feathers around the collar. Her bronze legs were straddled over a red velvet chair with her head leaning to the side letting her black wavy mane flow freely.

"*Aqui venida papi*," she murmured seductively to her client in Spanish as she motioned a perfectly French Manicured finger towards the gentleman to join her; as if he could.

Erika watched as Desire moved her hands slowly across her breasts pretending they were her client's hands exploring her body. Her nipples turned hard from the ice she began rubbing across them causing a trail of water to run down to her navel, then on to her thongless crotch.

I wish I was that ice. Her client typed.

Desire continued to taunt the man. Picking up another piece of ice she started rubbing it between her brown thighs to the inside of her pink sweetness until that piece melted away as well.

Zoom in closer baby and open up. I want to see all of you, the man added.

A movement in the corner of another entertainer's show caught her attention drawing her eyes away from Desire's private show. Amber, one of her new girls, was putting on a performance that was sure to keep her client hungering for more. She was in the corner of her room doing a number on a sex toy that would put Heather Hunter to shame. Erika chuckled to herself while she watched as Amber's head bobbed up and down, her mouth engulfing the toy…

A few months earlier

It had been a little over six months since Erika had her website *Fantasy Girls* up and running making the money she made at *Passionate Playmates* look like pocket change. She and Jade had started off as the main attractions quickly bringing in enough money, clientele, and new models that Erika decided to hang up her stilettos. Jade decided she wanted to try her hand at acting packed her bags and moved to Los Angeles in search of stardom. Erika wished her well reminding Jade she always had a home to come back to.

Erika ran the business from her house turning it into her main seduction lair. She had three rooms to allow modeling for girls who didn't have privacy in their own home. Shawn, her son, had his own room and she had so much extra space in her own room, that she turned part of it into her office for monitoring her employees.

Erika examined the woman sitting on the ivory leather couch in front of her. She had on a blue and gold Baby Phat Capri jump suit with matching wedged heel sandals. Her long red hair was pulled up in a sleek pony tail with a hump in the front. She sat on the couch across from Erika playing with her tongue ring waiting in anticipation for the interview to begin. Erika preferred to do all of her interviews in person so she had paid the potential model's expenses to come to her. She had contacted Erika through her Websites email. After she finished giving her the once over and reviewing the pictures Spice had handed her, Erika was ready to begin her questioning.

"So your stage name is Spice. What made you choose that name?" Erika asked looking directly at the girl.

"My sexy red hair of course!" she replied smiling as she flipped her hair over her shoulder for emphasis.

"I see and what is your nationality?" Erika inquired unaffected by Spice's attempt to be cute. Spice had very fair skin almost as pale as an albino but she obviously was not 100% White.

"Black and Irish my father is from Ireland and has red hair. Is that going to be a problem? You said you wanted all type of women," she said adjusting herself on the couch.

"It's for your profile *if* I decide to hire you. You can actually have two different profiles because we still do have clients that only prefer white women. A man would not even notice that you weren't White which is a plus. Now for the more serious questions, *what*, are you willing to do to entice a man to make him keep coming back for more?"

"Whatever they want me to," she said shrugging her arms.

"You need a much better answer than that if you want to be a *Fantasy Girl*," Erika replied annoyed. She was fed up with girls thinking that because they were cute men would just toss money at them. Erika knew for a fact men wanted something they felt they weren't getting at home.

"Well," she replied in a husky voice licking her bottom lip while moving closer to Erika, "I can show you." She stood up slowly rubbing her breasts through her top then slid one hand down her stomach, to the inside of her pants, and reached for Erika's hand with the other.

"What are you doing? I don't swing that way honey. As a matter of fact follow me," Erika said rising from her couch heading upstairs to one of the many private rooms in her home.

Opening the door, Erika pointed to the pink suede chaise in front of the computer and motioned for Spice to have a seat, and told her she will be right back. She flipped open her cell calling Kenny letting him know that Spice was ready. Erika headed down the hall towards her office to observe the show. She was just in time to see Spice's reaction to Kenny's face appearing on the screen asking her to show him what she was working with. Spice was a little hesitant before she started. She was searching around the room looking for something. Erika helped her out by pushing play on a CD that could be heard through the room's speakers.

Spice relaxed and proceeded to undress to the beat of the music. She slowly slid her top down almost if by accident, exposing her left breast, and then the right. As she rolled her hips she slid the rest of the outfit to the floor then she proceeded to climb on the chaise like tiger; slow and graceful. When she reached the other end of the chaise she spun around swinging her legs across the arm of the chair, lying upside down facing the camera. She put one finger in her mouth sucking on it with her glossy red lips as she slid her other hand down between her breasts past her navel, stopping once her hand was inside her red Victoria Secret thongs. She played with herself for a moment then removed her fingers showing the juice that flowed off them to the camera. In a forward flip motion she removed her thongs and landed with her rear end facing the camera. She exposed her pink nectar for Kenny to get an up close and personal view.

"You enjoy the show?" Erika asked after Spice was gone.

"Did I? You know I did, the question is what do you think Boss Lady?" Kenny said waiting patiently for her response.

"Well," Erika started, "she is hell of a lot better than the last three. Normally when I interview someone who works at a strip club they are so involved with dancing and doing tricks they don't connect to the client. They have to learn how to make the client feel as if they are with them in the room. Spice performed for you and you only. Heck if I was a man or bisexual I would have wanted her."

"So I guess that means she's hired."

"Yeah, but you know I won't call her to the end of the week to tell her. For some reason when I call them too early they act like they made this business and I need them. They even have the nerve to act like they are doing me a favor by logging on. Please, my name is Ecstasy, I can still put a man in a trance and make him cum his pants in less than a minute so they better recognize who the Queen Bee really is," Erika said upset that she allowed herself to get worked up again over firing some girls who were too Diva for the business last week.

"Okay, I'm on your side. Call the girl when you want to. By the way I just finished uploading the new photo's and the *Fantasy Girl of the Week*," he said not wanting to add fuel to the fire.

Jasmine and Sapphire somehow felt Erika should pay for their clothing as well as personal vacations outside of the ones she sent them on as groups to take photos for the website. Erika had a deal with a clothing designer that used to stop by the club selling her outfits to the dancers when Erika first started dancing. She extended the hefty discount to her girls as long as they bought three or more outfits at a time, and even gave them one free when they made the top five on the site. Her bending any further to please Jasmine and Sapphire was simply out of the question.

Erika even booked headline shows across the nation at various strip clubs that brought in major cash just because of her site. All they had to do was dance three songs for a flat fee. No lap dancing unless they wanted to for extra but she left the decision up to them. They did however; have to mingle with the clientele. Jasmine and Sapphire tried to treat Erika like she was a regular employee and not the owner because they were the fist ones hired. She quickly showed them who was in charge and let them go. Keeping them around only would have put ideas in the other girls' heads.

"Thanks, I will talk to you later, Asia's at the door," Erika replied disconnecting the call from Kenny.

Erika opened the door for Asia and watched as she switched past her wearing a pink Enyce sweat outfit with her Louis Vitton satchel in tow. After Erika informed Asia she was in the Love Nest for her shift, Asia continued her journey past Erika and up the stairs. Erika labeled the room the Love Nest because it was up to date with a 70s twist. The room had a big, crimson, round bed in the center. Round mirrors accented one of the walls, and a white love seat instead of a simple chair sat in front of the computer. There was even a silhouette board for the girls to stand behind to cast off a sexy shadow for building anticipation when they were changing for their client. The room had a black light and a lava lamp to complete the look. The men went wild when the girls would put on body paint and turn the black light on.

Asia was hands down one of Erika's best money makers. She was an exotic beauty mixed with Black, White, and Japanese; complemented by her long, thick, black, wavy hair, and almond shaped eyes. Her skin was a perfect bronze all year round. She could be the perfect stand-in for Kamora Lee, if it weren't for her piercing green eyes. She had luscious lips just like her and the body to match. She was one of the most requested models and also the most downloaded in the picture gallery. A sweet plus of being online is that several men could pay to watch her at the same time instead of having to wait, risking them loosing interest and going to another site.

Asia's performance in her shows had up to thirty-two men watching her at the same time one evening. Thirty-two men paying $20 for fifteen minutes that was $640 for one show and she rarely did less than ten a night. Chics in a strip club would collapse trying to do thirty-two lap dances in a night, not even coming close to the $3000 that Asia was guaranteed to make on one of her bad days. She was definitely a gold mine, always finding ways to keep them yearning for more.

Erika sniffed the perfume Asia left lingering in the air after she headed up the stairs to prepare for her eagerly waiting clients. Even though it was barely 2:00 pm, Erika knew people will want to see their idea of a fantasy. Erika laughed at the idea of some corporate big wig sitting in his office getting his fantasy fulfilled prior to going into a meeting, while making sure his employees computers were monitored by fire walls blocking sites like hers.

Normally Erika would have went to her office to monitor a few more shows but today she needed to finish up two other interviews, hire security guards, and check on a building downtown that was for sale. She decided to get security guards once she opened up her home to allow her models to work out of it. She didn't want to risk anyone daring to come in her home even though she had cameras all around the house. She shuttered at the thought of the shooting at *Passionate Playmates*, her old employer, several months prior.

Slamming the door after dealing with the last interview, Erika almost lost it. She was an equal opportunist but some people needed their asses kicked. It was one thing for someone to use a fake picture online when they were not going to see a person face to face, but what in the world would posses a normal person to use a fake picture knowing they were going to an interview. She had no problem with gay men dressing like women, however, this man could not have been a woman no mater how much money he paid for it. He/she was a linebacker wearing a leopard printed dress that was spray painted on and *It* had a full beard. What Erika had just witnessed was worse than Wesley Snipes and Patrick Swayze combined in that old movie *To Wong Fu.* She felt like she was on the show *Punked* and Ashton was about to show up at any moment during the grueling interview to tell her it was a joke. The interview only lasted five minutes but it felt more like forty to Erika. The picture Erika had seen online was a beautiful blond that reminded her of Jade. This monster had blond hair alright but he was no where near a Jade look-alike. He/she wasn't even the same nationality. Erika could only imagine who he/she used to talk on the phone to her when she scheduled the interview because the person who just left sounded like James Earl Jones, when he was the voice of Darth Vader. She would have preferred Star Jones after her gastric bypass surgery with all the sagging skin hanging.

Erika leaned on the door counting to ten when the doorbell rang again. “Please tell me *It* did not forget something,” Erika sighed, snatching open the door to a sexy piece of eye candy. A 6 ft 1 in, bald headed, dark brown piece of chocolate man was standing at the door. He had on a blue polo shirt with khaki’s and a body that had not missed a day at the gym. Erika had just found a replacement to her dream husband Dwayne Johnson a.k.a. the Roc.

“Can I help you?” Erika managed to get out before she could get lost in those big brown eyes.

“Hi, I’m Xavier. I’m with the security company,” he said smiling displaying a dimple in his left cheek.

“I’m Erika and you’re twenty minutes early,” she replied looking at her watch. She prayed he was not a brotha on the down low. She had read those books by E. Lynn Harris, causing her to suspect almost every fine muscular man. For all she knew this could be that Basil character he wrote about.

“Better to be early, than not on time. CP time is for people who really do not want to be there in the first place,” Xavier replied showing his almost perfect teeth.

"Well, come on in and have a seat," Erika said leading him to her formal dinning room that she had decorated with Oriental artwork. Her father used to be in the Navy and always brought her back things when he went to Korea, Japan, the Philippines or wherever his ship took him. The room had a two-inch thick glass dinning table with burgundy leather chairs from Ashley Furniture that could seat up to nine people. A burgundy glass vase with cream flowers was her center piece. A large gold and burgundy Korean fan was on one wall and a 3 foot long picture with the Asian letters for Love, Prosperity, and Wealth was on the opposite side. In the corner of the room sat a large gold Happy Prophet, which most people confused as a Buda, on top of a dark cherry wood stand with a dragon on the front. She was even lucky enough to have found Asian writing border matching her colors.

"Nice room, I see you took a lot of time with it," Xavier commented taking a seat on the right side of the room after he noticed Erika's paperwork already sitting at the head of the table.

"Would you like anything to drink? Water, tea, or Pepsi?" Erika asked, wanting to get away for a moment to compose herself before she would be able conduct business. He opted for water, sending Erika to the kitchen before he could see the drool forming in the corner of her mouth. She licked her lips at the eye candy as she walked away.

Erika was glad she chose to conduct the security interviews in a more professional manner than she had for the models. There was no way in the world she would have been comfortable sitting on her couch next to him.

Taking a deep breath to relax, Erika returned to the room in full business mode. She asked him several questions about his previous employers, as well as his opinions about her business. She noticed that he had played professional football for two years. He told her that he was an ex-running back for the Raiders and injured his knee landing wrong after a tackle. Figuring all of his information was easily verifiable; Erika decided to extend him an offer of employment. She would contact the company regarding their fees.

"I have to a confession to make," Xavier said with a serious look on his face.

"Yes," she replied thinking, "*what the hell now.*"

"I own the company. You don't need to contact them," he said handing her a business card with his name as the CEO. "After I left the NFL this was something I decided to invest in."

"Then what the heck was all of this about?"

"I actually conduct all of my interviews to make sure we are dealing with a legit company. My employees are not some club bouncers. They are more on the line of body guards. Even though I have it in black and white on my website, people still try to hire us for their clubs anyway. With a name like Fantasy Girls I had to be sure. Besides, what man in his right mind would pass up an opportunity to meet with the owner of a business like this? I do fill in for my workers from time to time as well." Just as he said that one of her models stuck her head in the room waving to Erika letting her know she was leaving for the day. Erika looked at her watch and realized that almost two hours had past while she had been interviewing Mr. Sexy Ex NFL Player.

Erika let her model's make up their own schedules. Her only stipulation was they had to turn them in a week in advance so she or her sister, Keisha would be there. Keisha moved in with a couple of other college students, but still came by the house almost every day. Once she had security she wouldn't have to worry about the models as much. She could just watch the tapes later to see if any thing out the ordinary had happened.

After Xavier watched Vixen walk out the door, he had a few questions for Erika himself. He asked her how many models she had, how many would be in the house at a time, and how late they would be required to stay in the evenings to walk the models out. She explained that because this was a residential area she did not want security hanging out around the outside of the house. They could monitor them on the cameras. No clients were coming to her house any way. She had stop sending her girls to bachelor parties unless they were for the higher society because no one else wanted to pay her decent rates but they wanted the girls to put in overtime expecting sexual favors.

Xavier gave Erika a copy of his contract so she can give it to her lawyer to look over. Erika's lawyer was actually only a paralegal and her sister, but hey if she could prepare a brief for a lawyer, then she was good enough to read Erika's documents.

Once she said goodbye to Xavier and assuring him she would call after she reviewed the contract with her lawyer Erika headed to the kitchen to cook her, her son and the night crew dinner. The girls normally ate before they came or brought their own food but for some reason when she cooked the smell would bring their watering mouths to the kitchen begging.

Keisha brought Shawn home from pre-kindergarten just as the smell from her lemon baked chicken started filling the air.

"Mommy!" Shawn sang running into the kitchen.

"Shawn!" She sang back smiling at him in his green kiddy Coogi shirt and jeans with his white and green matching Nike's.

"The teacher said he is so helpful in class. So helpful that he is starting to do the other kids work for them," Keisha said lifting the top off one of the pots on the stove.

"Aww man. I guess I need to have a little talk with him. It will be done in about 30 minutes. Go relax." Erika said turning her attention back to Shawn.

She asked him about his day at school, which he described in great detail. When he was finished, she kissed him on the cheek; sending him outside to play on his swing set.

Chapter 2

Heather stuck her tongue out at the other girls as she grabbed her client by the arm and led him to her room. She had been feeling like an outcast since the day she had stepped foot in Nevada. She lied to Ecstasy telling her that she was working at the Bunny Ranch, when in reality she was being pimped out at a truck stop hotel. The guy Heather and her sister met online pretended to be part of the Bunny Ranch, paying for her and her sister to fly to Nevada. When they arrived at the baggage claim, they saw a handsome Italian man wearing a sleek black Armani business suit. He was talking on his cell phone, waiting for them. After he gathered their luggage he led them to a silver Mercedes intriguing them with his charming looks and charisma as he drove them to a hotel. He told Heather and her sister that he wanted them to get freshened up and fed before their big interview. Once they were inside he asked for their identification, saying it was needed for taxes.

After he left two bigger men came in the room gathering up their cell phones, money, and credit cards. Grabbing Heather by the wrists they dragged her to a tinted dark blue SUV and tossed her in the back seat. Before Heather realized what was happening to her she was on her way to a different hotel; away from her sister and all of her personal her belongings.

After what felt like hours they finally arrived at the other hotel. Heather was carried from the truck to a side door of the hotel and shoved in a room with the door shutting firmly behind her. A man was sitting in a wooden chair placed in the center of the room, between the bed and nightstand. He told her to come closer and make him want her. Heather began to perform like she had at *Passionate Playmates*. She began swaying her hips from side to side humming a tune to drown out the uncomfortable silence. Moving a little closer she rubbed her breasts in his face. The man looked at her and yawned. Confused by his lack of interest in her dancing she asked what she could do. Glaring at her he said, “You’re going to let me fuck you senseless because that’s what I paid for.”

Realization hitting her, she made a dash for the door. “Noooo,” she wailed halted in her tracks by one of the men who brought her there. He showed her his gun and pointed to the bed. Realizing she was trapped Heather lay on the bed ready to endure what she knew was to come. When he was finished he took $300 and tossed it on top of her. That was the first time she was prostituted out but not the last.

A few men later, Heather, was no longer an amateur. She began taking complete control once she was in the privacy of the hotel room. She was determined to make enough money to get back to her family. Her Pimp took everything she earned claiming that she didn't need money because he took care of her. The other girls may have fallen for that line but she had known a better life. Most of the other girls were straight out of high school or maybe even younger. Heather pinched off ten and twenty dollars whenever she thought she could get away with it, she hid her money in the bathroom ceiling tile when she was supposed to be washing up.

The men that came to the hotel could care less if she performed for them, they wanted a quick release. She cursed Ecstasy for not even offering her a job on her new website when she called her shortly after arriving in town. Her pimp made Heather make calls to her family and friends twice a week so no one would be suspicious. With every blowjob, hand job, and man she let inside her, her hatred grew. She preferred giving blowjobs over letting men penetrate her. If she did it good enough her torture would be over in less than five minutes; which is what she was planning on doing with this John. Pushing him on the floor she unzipped his pants, pulled out his goods, and began to suck him dry.

"Slow down baby," he grunted as he tried to refrain from releasing too soon. Heather blocked out his cries to slow down and began stroking his member harder and faster. The sounds coming from him quickly turned to pleasure. She turned her face to the side just before he came; finishing him off in less than three minutes. Snatching the money off the dresser, she escorted him back out of the hotel and returned to the room to gargle with Listerine before heading to the front lobby in search of another client.

Heather knew better than to linger between clients. The girls got beat if they didn't have as many clients as their Pimp thought they should, or if they didn't try. Heather learned that the hard way on her first day. Right after her first encounter she came out the room trying to be invisible when she saw the other prostitutes' line up to flaunt their stuff for the men coming in the hotel. When she ignored three men in a row, her Pimp showed up, punching her in the stomach, right in front of the other girls. Heather held her stomach as she fell to the floor. Gripping a fist full of hair he jerked her back to her feet. Inches away from her face he whispered to her to get her lazy ass back to work or death would be the least of her worries. Before he walked back out the hotel he kissed her on the forehead, informing her that the only reason he had chosen the stomach was so he wouldn't damage her pretty face.

***

Erika and Xavier came to terms with their contract after a few minor changes deciding on two security guards per day, following her *Fantasy Girls* schedules. With more and more home invasions going on across the city, Erika was glad she had the extra protection.

"And our top story for the hour, a family was playing cards with friends when men ran in their house, robbing them; injuring three people and killing another…" the Channel 6 news anchor woman was saying. Erika grimaced at the television; turning it off. She was still dealing with visions of seeing someone she was close to dead from a gunshot wound, with his body slumped over a chair*;* to take any chances in her own home.

Once Ryan arrived for his shift Erika left to go to her appointment with her realtor regarding the property downtown. The building was only one block away from the *Red Garter Strip Club* on Illinois Street so she knew the area was properly zoned. Excitement flowing through her, she sang along to the music playing on her iPOD as her Charger zig zagged between the rush hour traffic. She also had a fully loaded Cadillac Escalade but she only chose to drive it when she had her son with her. It was easier than having to deal with the stares of people watching her get out of a big truck alone, as high as the gas prices were. She was hearing more often about people opting to ride the city bus. Erika often wondered why as big as Indianapolis was, there wasn't a better transit system. There should be a subway, monorail, anything but just a city bus. The city bus would take you all the way downtown, make you change buses, just to bring you all the way back to your side of town, before dropping you off five blocks from where you started in the first place .

"The head *Fantasy Girl* won't be caught dead on the bus next to the crack heads and babies with rotten pampers," Erika said, winking at herself in the review mirror. She had enough of that experience a few years earlier when her car broke down and she couldn't afford to get it fixed right away. She was working a temp job at the time so the bus was her only option. The bus was so packed she ended up being smashed next to a woman holding a baby whose pamper smelled like he took a dump two weeks ago; not to mention the mother's body odor was just as foul. To make matters worse a crack head kept walking up and down the aisle harassing people.

"Gimme $2 for this PSP," he said breathing on the back of someone's neck. The PSP screen was cracked and the back was held together with a rubber band. "You got a dollar? How about some change?" he was saying displaying his rotten teeth moving in her direction with a huge pee stain on his pants. Closing her eyes she pretended to sleep for the rest of the ride downtown. He ignored her continuing down the aisle. She endured episodes like that for a month before she could afford to pay for her car repairs.

The weather was so nice she wished she had decided to ride her Ducati motorcycle. She had joined a bike club, *Indy Hot Girls*, a few months earlier after talking to one of their founders on *MySpace*. She loved the look on people's faces when she pulled up on her ride. Most females rode on the back as a passenger, or if they rode solo they as looked harder than some men.

Shayla was already outside of her Ivory Tahoe walking around inspecting the building when Erika pulled up. She had informed Erika prior to scheduling an appointment that the building had been on the market for over a year so she could definitely get the price reduced.

"Nice rims. When did you get them?" Shayla asked checking out Erika's upgrades to her car.

"I ordered them a week ago. They came in yesterday. What do you think so far?" Erika replied noticing how nice her old college roommate looked in her baby blue Dolce and Gabana business suit. Shayla had been a trend setter since college. She would take an outfit that Erika thought was ugly and make it look beautiful. She even picked out a few items for Erika, in which, she would not have purchased even if Mr. Armani himself designed it just for her.

"The structure isn't bad but I will not give it a thumbs up until I see how well they kept it up inside," Shayla said over her shoulder, as she punched in a code on a keypad attached to the building door.

It was an old warehouse but it appeared to have several new renovations. This was something Erika felt she could work with. The Colts new stadium, that would soon be hosting the Super Bowl, could be seen off in the distance and would bring in extra patrons.

Shayla walked around knocking on walls, shaking pipes, and testing the stairs giving the building a thorough inspection. She made sure to check every inch of it from the structure itself to the plumbing before she finally gave it mid-thumbs up little over an hour later.

Dusting off her hands she commented, “There were a few things I want to discuss with the seller before putting in a bid for you to purchase it.”

“Hey, that’s what I’m paying you the big bucks for,” Erika joked. Shayla refused any direct payment. She made money off the sale.

Coming out the building Erika nudged Shayla, getting her attention to look in the direction of a stripper going into the back door of the *Red Garter,* a popular downtown gentleman’s club.

“She better go make that money to pay for the Colts new stadium, I mean those property taxes, that were some how mysteriously inflated,” Shayla said joking about the outrageous property tax increase.

“Well she better do more than some shaking up in there if she wants to pay those,” Erika said still ticked off at the increase on hers. She could more than afford the increase but the fact that they went up almost 120% still has her eyes sore from popping out her head when she opened her mail.

“On a more serious note,” Shayla said changing the subject. “I am so proud of you. You have always been a hustler when it came to getting what you want and taking care of business, even if it was something as simple as convincing me to walk up to a prison to get out of the cold."

"Thanks girl, and no you didn't bring that up. That is a pre-Ecstasy tales of the broke experience!"

Erika was still laughing as she got in her car thinking about her college days at Indiana State University. Erika had heard about a party at Vincennes University and convinced Shayla to go. After driving 45 minutes they got to the party and it was nothing more than a group of guys they knew smoking marijuana and drinking. The girls were pissed off at first but after a few drinks of their favorite drink at the time, *Truce,* a mixture of several different Vodka's, with a fruity taste, they were having a good time. Erika didn't smoke the Blunts they were passing around because of her scholarship and the jitters she got when she had tried it a few years prior. Plus, it appeared to make her friends act lazy. Instead, she sat around with her drink in one hand and a Black and Mild in the other.

After the makeshift party with the guys acting like they were rap stars, making up weak lyrics, and the girls dancing in the background like video chics, they decided to head back to ISU for a real party. They had driven about twenty minutes when Erika's check engine light came on and the car started slowing down to a crawl. Erika pulled the car off to the side of the road just before it completely died and they were crushed by a semi truck. This wasn't the first time the car had issues; heck she drove without breaks for almost six months stopping by pulling up the emergency break. Her car was purely drive at your own risk, but her black and red 10 year old Beretta was her baby.

"Shit!" Erika said smacking the steering wheel.

"Well we could walk to the nearest gas station, or we can wait until a truck driver came by, show him some skin, and take his truck," Shayla said with a straight face.

"Shayla,"

"What?"

"Shut your high ass up," replied Erika. She normally got a kick out of her when she was high because she always said the funniest things, but this was not the time.

It was the middle of January in Indiana so the temperature was at the highest 15 degrees not to mention it was snowing earlier in the day. Sobering up, Erika checked out their surroundings. She vaguely remembered an exit a few miles back, but the prison they were in front of looked rather inviting. Well maybe she really hadn't sobered up that much to think that a prison was inviting, she reasoned. With little effort she convinced Shayla to walk up to the guard gate with her so they could at least use the phone. The area they were in was a dead zone, rendering their prepaid cell phones useless.

Paranoid from the marijuana smoking, Shayla began talking about conspiracy theories on why there were more Black Men in prison than there were in college. It was a government design in place to destroy the community and the Black family. She covered everything but the real issue on how it was their fault for doing the crime in the first place. Erika barely paid her any attention because she was too busy fighting the strong gusts of wind. The wind was so strong it blew her car door backwards when she opened it, making it hard to close. It was so cold it felt as though her nose hairs had turned to ice. Her eyes starting to water she turned her head to the side trying to avoid direct contact from the wind. Their frozen faces seemed as if they would shatter with each step they made.

Before they even got close to the guard station a big spotlight was on them and they heard a loud voice over a speaker.

"Come any closer and we will shoot!"

"Well you are going to have to shoot me then because it is fucking cold out here and we have no where else to go!" Erika screamed back at the voice flipping him off at the same time. Vodka seemed to give her a set of extra large balls at times or it could have been the cold freezing her brain, she couldn't really remember.

After the guards got tired of Erika cussing them out and not moving they opened the gate and a car came out. A guard said that his shift had ended and he would give them a ride back to Terre Haute. Shayla started talking about him being a serial killer stealing a guard's car to come out and get them. Ignoring Shayla's paranoia, Erika pushed her in the car bumping her head against the door.

Erika smiled in disbelief reminiscing over her college days as she pulled up in her driveway of her two storey light blue home. A black Cadillac Escalade was parked on the street in front of the empty lot next to her house, exactly where she instructed her security to park.

The front door to her house swung open before she had a chance to turn the handle. Xavier was standing there looking edible in his khaki pants and blue polo shirt with his company's logo on the upper right side.

"What are you doing opening up my door?" Erika said putting her hands on her hips pretending like she was mad.

"It is my shift, remember I told you I work some shifts," he answered stepping closer, invading her personal space.

"Whatever, move please," she said moving past him taking in his masculine physique. Erika had to get herself together quick before she pulled him out to the garage, and showed him why she was called Ecstasy. His muscles on his arms were calling out for her to let him grab her, and pin her up against the wall, as she wrapped her long legs around his waist ready for whatever he was going to give her.

"…so I hope you don't mind," Xavier finished.

"Don't mind what," she said snapping back to reality. "I'm sorry. I have a few things on my mind."

"So I see," he replied looking at her with a smirk on his face. "I said I went ahead and made dinner for you and Shawn, where is he?"

"He's spending the weekend with his aunt. You cooked?"

Walking into the kitchen her senses were assaulted by the smell of spices and herbs. She tried to sneak a peak in the pots but he swatted her hands away.

"Smells good, what is it?" She inquired.

"Lamb, mixed vegetables, and wild rice. I'm sure one of the girls will gladly eat his portion. Kind of glad Shawn won't be here. I would love to get to know you better since my shift does not end until 4:00am," he replied.

"Lamb? Wow, there's a lot more to you than I thought," she said disregarding the last part of his statement. She had no intention of staying up late with the man that made the inner sweetness between her thighs twitch just by looking at her. It had been months since her last encounter with Mario, some guy she met in the club when she had one too many drinks, and started getting turned on by all the grinding they were doing on the dance floor. Once the deed was done she slipped out his house like a thief in the night. Xavier on the other hand, had her feeling like a lioness stalking her prey, ready to rip his clothes off, and make him scream her name, right on her glass table.

"The food will be ready in a minute," he said interrupting her naughty thoughts.

Erika watched as he walked over to the oven lifting the lids off the pots; inspecting his work. "Sexy and he can cook! I'm in love," she thought observing how at home he seemed in the kitchen, while still keeping his eyes on the new monitors Erika had installed; allowing her to be able to see the girls from downstairs as well as from her office.

Chapter 3

"Finally!" Jade exclaimed hanging up her pink Baby Phat cell phone. She had been in Los Angeles for nearly five months, going from audition to audition without so much as a call back. Jade's perfectly tanned body with her blond hair and eyes as blue as the ocean were a show-stopper back home, but in LA it barely got her a second glance. Her fake boobs were nothing compared to what other people she met had endured under the knife to achieve Hollywood's vision of perfection. She heard of lipo, tummy tucks, and nose jobs but was not ready for people who allowed themselves to have the point of their ears removed, triceps implanted, chins implanted, wrinkles in their forehead removed, hips shaved, and even changing the shape of their belly button. People had literally turned themselves into Ken and Barbie.

Andres St. Jean introduced himself to her at the mall as a movie producer. She was paying more attention to his accent than what he was actually saying, until he said he wanted to have Jade read for a part in a new horror movie he was producing. Shifting her Forever 21 bags to one hand she had to refrain from snatching the black and gold business card he was holding out of his hand. Andres said he thought she would be perfect to play the part of the leading male's girlfriend. She hated how most females were portrayed in horror movies, but to get her foot in the door, she would play the young dumb girl running from a serial killer, through the woods, and tripping over her own feet, so she could become the killer's next victim. Heck she could die ten minutes into the movie as long as her face was seen.

Jade watched as Andres walked away in his gray Sean Jean suit. "Casting agency's always said they would call and never did so why would this be any different," she reasoned, putting the card in her back pocket continuing her shopping. Victoria Secrets was having their semi-annual sale and she wouldn't be stuck sorting through the leftovers.

Exhausted from all of the shopping, Jade headed back to her one bedroom loft. She barely had one heel in the door when she felt her cell vibrating in her purse. Dropping her bags she whipped out her phone. 'Private Caller' showed on her screen making her to answer with caution.

"Hello," she said slowly.

"Jade?" a thick accent inquired.

"Yes."

"This is Andres St. Jean. I know this is short notice but one of our girls fell ill. Will it be possible for you to make it to an audition today?"

"Why of course! When and where do I need to be?" she questioned trying to maintain her excitement. Giving her the time and directions he ended the call.

She had just received the call she was waiting for, not wasting any time Jade tore through her closet looking for the perfect outfit to wear to her audition. Finally deciding on a turquoise Bebe satin halter top, trimmed in white to highlight her perky breasts, white DKNY Capri pants, and matching Jimmy Choo stilettos, she picked up her Marc Jacob's bag and Chanel shades heading out the door to meet her destiny.

Jade pulled up in front of the Hilton in her gold Range Rover with ten minutes to spare. She took notice of the upscale businessmen and women socializing among one another, as she searched for the small conference room sign. Steadying her nerves she put on a professional demeanor before walking in the door.

"Jade! So glad you could make it in such a short notice," Andres said over exaggerating his words.

"Thank you for the opportunity. I'm sure I will not make you regret it," she replied with confidence.

"Have a seat so we can get down to business," he said pulling out a chair and handing her a script.

Jade scanned the script observing how cheesy it was, but gave it her best performance anyway. She wasn't Jessica Alba just yet; to begin complaining about any role she was offered. Jade would have read off the side of a cereal box for a chance at stardom. Besides, plenty of actors played cheesy roles before getting their big break.

"That was great. Production starts on Thursday. Will you be ready?"

"Excuse me? I mean yes I will be ready. Thank you," she answered trying to hide her shock. She was finally on her way.

Andres gave her all the information she needed to start. Jade had one scene so she would only be paid $500; which was fine with her. It wasn't about the money just yet.

***

After they ate the delicious meal Xavier had prepared they moved to the living room and started watching, *Perfect Stranger,* a movie starring Halle Berry and Bruce Willis. Feeling more comfortable with Xavier after their great dinner conversation Erika sat next to him laying her head on his shoulder.

Xavier watched as Erika closed her eyes drifting off to sleep.

“Damn she is sexy,” he thought kissing her on the forehead. Erika let out a soft moan adjusting her head so her lips were just inches away from his.

He couldn’t resist those soft looking lips any longer. Leaning closer he gave her a soft kiss on the lips. When she opened her eyes and smiled he dove in ravaging her lips and tongue. Turned on by his kisses Erika returned his passion with a fire of her own.

Xavier picked her up carrying her to the backyard patio. The yard had a privacy fence so no one would see what they were about to do. He positioned her down on a reclining lounge chair continuing to kiss her and lick on her neck. He lifted up her shirt so he could suck freely on her ample breasts. Her nipples were so hard they were standing at attention, like two good soldiers as he moved from one another. He started making a trail of kisses down her stomach, past her belly button, continuing on to her sweetness, while he slid off her pants at the same time.

Once her fruit was exposed Xavier dived in sucking and licking on her clit, making her juices flow. Erika was on the verge of loosing her mind grabbing his bald head pushing him in deeper as she wrapped her athletic legs around his shoulders, giving in to the ecstasy.

Erika murmured, “Eat this, you know you want it….ooh shit I’m about to cum,” as she released all over his face.

“Wake up sleepy head the movie’s over.”

“Huh,” she replied confused as she set up on the couch.

“You fell asleep and the movie is over. You should go get in your bed to get some rest while I get caught up on the shows I missed,” he replied, ushering her off to her room.

“Yeah, I guess you’re right,” Erika replied still dazed. “Goodnight and thanks for cooking.”

“You’re welcome,” he mouthed gently shutting her door.

Erika was dumbfounded she couldn’t believe she dreamed all of that. She checked her underwear realizing they were soaked from her all too real wet dream. “Wow if he can make me cum in a dream I can’t wait to feel the real thing,” she thought stepping into the shower ready to replay her dream all over again with a little help from her favorite sex toy.

She learned the art of masturbating working at *Passionate Playmates* after about a month or so. She was tired of performing for men night after night without getting something out of it, so she decided to implore some skills she read in a book about women knowing their bodies. What could it hurt, she was already naked pretending to have orgasms anyway. Erika stood over her client who was sitting on a leather couch, giving him a peak of her pink flower, letting her fingers go to work until she came for the first time on her own. He even gave her an extra $50 on top of the $300 he had already placed in her tip tray to show his gratitude. She had been a frequent self pleaser ever since.

Xavier would blush if he knew the things Erika had him doing in her mind. She fell asleep dreaming about turning him out.

The next morning Erika woke up refreshed. Shayla left a voice message bright and early with good news about the building. The company had accepted the price she offered. They were so happy to finally have someone take it off their hands after sitting on the market for almost a year. She was about to become the proud owner of a Martini Bar with private rooms for men and women who wanted a little company. She searched through her cell phone looking for the number of the contractor she met at Lowe's, a few weeks earlier, when she was trying to figure out what color she wanted to paint her son's room.

The contractor told her to email him exactly what her vision was and he would get back to her with a price within a few days. After sending the email off, Erika got dressed so she could conduct an interview with a girl, named Amber, that Ryan, one of the security guards, had sent her way a week prior. Erika was tired of the stripper chics with attitudes she seemed to keep running into, but after Spice's performance she was willing to give it a chance.

Amber showed up at her house at exactly 10:30am looking like an innocent college girl. She wore a black Von Dutch tank top, a pair of Seven Jeans and a Colgate smile. Erika liked her instantly. She was confident without being cocky. She replied to every question with a well thought out answer letting Erika know she took the interview seriously, and her practice show was amazing. She knew exactly how to play to the camera. She drew the man in, making him yearn for more, instead acting like; *I can't wait until this jerk leaves so I can get my $20 off this lap dance*.

"What would you say if I said you were hired?" Erika asked hypothetically breaking her own rules on hiring girls after their interview.

"When can I start?" Amber grinned.

"Great, I have a photo shoot planned for tomorrow in Atlanta. Are you available?"

"What time does the bus leave?"

"*Fantasy Girls* don't do Greyhound. They fly unless they want to drive their own vehicle. Kenny will call you with all the details in a few hours."

Kenny was doing such a wonderful job keeping up with the site that Erika was going to make sure he knew it by taking him to his favorite restaurant, Rick's Boatyard, later on that evening for an early dinner once she finished calculating her business earnings. Erika hated doing the bills but there was no way she was about to pay an accountant to steal from her. She saw how the stars were always getting in trouble about their finances because of other people. She alone handled the books and made sure Uncle Sam got his cut.

Erika sat at her cherry Oakwood desk deducting out site maintenance for Kenny, security, and the girls pay, in which they moaned and groaned about getting a check instead of cash until they saw $8000 or more for the month. She tallied her earnings to more than $70,000 for the month. Business was definitely doing well.

Erika was still amazed to see how many people would go online to get their freak on. She was way more generous than most in the adult entertainment business. She took 30% off the girls shows but also covered their numerous and always updated photos to include travel and hotel costs. She even used her marketing skills to promote the girls as headliners in numerous clubs around the country and did not care if they worked other side gigs.

Everything was falling into place for Erika. She had more than enough to pay for a more secluded house up in Geist, an area where the wealthier lived. She didn't consider it elite living because she heard of a few drug dealers owning property in that area as well. She could even afford to put down a huge deposit on her new building downtown. The only thing missing from the equation was her girl Jade there to run the business with her. She was definitely missing her best friend who she realized hadn't bother to call in the past week even after Erika left her several messages. It was very strange for Jade not to call at least twice a week, especially after she had her first acting job.

"Maybe the job has her working long hours and she's tired," Erika reasoned.

Chapter 4

The bourgeois waiter showed them to a small table located in the back corner of the restaurant. Erika sat across from Kenny at the table checking out his linen outfit and freshly manicured nails. She admired how he dressed not quite hip hop but not uptight either. He was always nice and professional when he was around her. As a matter of fact, the only time Erika could ever recall him even joking around with her is when he was on the phone.

"Something to drink?" The waiter huffed at them like he had some place more important to be.

"Heineken for me and the lady will have a Pomegranate Martini please. We are also ready to order if you do not mind," said Kenny. He wasn't about to let the waiter get away from them. It had already taken him 20 minutes just to take their drink order.

Taking their order, the waiter speed walked back off in the direction of the kitchen leaving them alone in silence.

Noticing Kenny was being extra quiet she decided to break the ice.

"I just want you to know I appreciate everything you have done for me. Without you I don't think my business would be as successful," she started. "The constant updates you do on the pictures and designs keep the men wanting more. I think they come back just to see what's new."

"Me, no you are the one with the vision and I admire that. You are a hard working, dedicated, and independent woman. You saw something you wanted and went for it," he replied in his British accent she had finally become accustomed to. It wasn't his fault but every time he spoke she still had a image of Jeffrey from the old TV show, *The Fresh Prince of Bel Air,* starring Will Smith.

"Gee thanks, but this dinner is about your great work. You're my right hand man. I don't know what I would do without you," she said pulling out a cashiers check from her purse. "Here is a bonus for you."

Erika slid the check written out for $5,000 across the table to him. Kenny stared at it for a moment before speaking.

"One day you will see that it's not the money that keeps me around. Any way let's eat," he said changing the subject as the waiter placed their food on the table. Without saying a word, the waiter turned and marched away.

Looking at the roasted duck, asparagus, and mashed potatoes, Erika forgot what she was about to say. Her stomach growled at the sight in front of her.

It was like pulling teeth but Erika eventually got Kenny to loosen up as they ate their meal. She got him to talk about his family and life growing up in London. She enjoyed seeing this side of him and not the stuffy and boring person she had come to know. The conversation was going so well they ended up talking for over an hour after the waiter cleared their plates and left the check.

"Will there be anything else?" the waiter asked with annoyance for the third time in less than 5 minutes.

"I take it that's the hint for us to leave?" Erika shot back looking him up and down.

"Well, we do have other customers waiting," he said reaching across her clearing the table.

"Well why are you just now saying so instead of pacing back and forth like we are up to no good? I notice you did not bother the other party who arrived at the same time we did," Kenny added.

"Do you know who that is?" he whispered like he was about to give them classified information. "That is the owner of the Colts."

"So freaking what! We are paying just like he is. Forget it, before you drive me to act ignorant up in here. That would be what you would consider ghetto because you have never actually been to the ghetto to comprehend the true meaning," Erika hissed rising up out of her chair making a bee line to the door.

"Wait up," Kenny said catching up to her. "That idiot really hit a nerve I see."

"Yeah, people like him always want your money but don't want you to be seen. Did you even notice how he walked us to a freaking corner table right next to the restrooms when there were plenty others in the middle of the restaurant? And how he kept guiding me towards the cheaper items on the menu? And how long it took him to even take our order in the first place? Not to mention the funky comment he mumbled after taking our order. The whole he knows how "we" never tip well so why even bother. Hell, I always tip very well. I mean if the waiter does there job, like coming to the table and acknowledging our presence! You know what…never mind. I don't feel like getting my blood pressure up and going back in their cussing his simple tail out!"

"As you would say, you are a hot mess," Kenny said laughing, "even if everything you just said was true."

After they said their goodbyes she was still trying to figure him out. She came to the conclusion on her way home that the reason he was so boring was because he didn't have a woman in his life. She was so deep in thought she did not notice the gold Mustang parked across the street when she pulled in the garage.

Once she was in the comforts of her home and settled the doorbell rang. No other girls were on the schedule this evening and Keisha was out of town. Turning off her bathwater she walked downstairs not bothering to look at her security cameras.

"This better be important to be interrupting my piece and quiet," she said to the person on the other side of the door before she opened it.

"Jade? Girl! What are you doing here?" she screamed hugging her friend. "I thought you were on your way to glamour and glitz with your first acting role?"

"I was, man I don't even know where to begin," Jade sighed flopping down on a black leather couch in the living room.

Kicking off her shoes, Jade leaned back on the arm of the couch like she was in a therapist office and began to explain what happened. She described how she showed up for her first day on the set ready and willing to dive completely into her character. She studied her few lines the night before and knew that the deranged killer was supposed to make her his next victim while she was having intercourse with her boyfriend, in the back of his truck, in an isolated park. After she was in her under garments the director told her he wanted it to be more realistic and could she please remove her clothes. She wasn't very comfortable, but it was just an act. Things got really strange when her co-star showed up in a robe, dropped it to the floor, and slid next to her in the truck asking her if his Johnson was big enough for her. If that wasn't bad enough the director was trying to coax her into different sexual positions like she was just going to have sex right there on the spot. When she kept refusing, the co-star got pissed off.

"Andres I know you wanted to make an amateur porn film, but did you have to get a damn virgin?" He said snatching up his robe walking off the set.

At the mention of porn Jade put her clothes back on with lightning speed and got the heck out of there. She was so mad she went back to her apartment, packed up her belongings, and drove home. It had taken her almost 2 ½ days to drive back to Indiana.

"Wow! That was crazy!" Erika responded, shaking her head in disbelief. "I think you need a drink."

She proceeded to the kitchen where she pulled out her blender whipping up some Pink Panties, a mix drink she learned in college. Vodka, pink lemonade, and whip cream. Handing Jade a drink they continued their conversation.

"So you were about to be a porn star?"

"What the hell ever, smarty? I can make more money working for you. Can you believe those bastards were only paying $500 to film me having sex?"

"The sad part is I bet they actually get a lot of people to do it, otherwise I don't think that guy would have ever approached you."

"I mean dang, they tried to act like it wasn't even porn. They tried to make it seem normal. Andres, the so called producer kept trying to ease me into letting some strange man have his way with me. If that's what the glamorous life is about then they can keep it," Jade said holding out her cup for a refill.

Filling her cup back up Erika replied, "You know you will always be a glamour girl to me. I told you before, you are my girl. You always have a home with me."

"I know, but *Fantasy Girls* is your baby. I need to find my own way and now I know that it isn't as an actress. I think I'm going to finish up school and that ain't free so when can I be put on the schedule boss?"

"Boss, I'm your girl, not your boss. I will put you on, but what you make you get, you won't be hurting me any," Erika replied. "Besides, school isn't cheap."

"You got that right, let me see my competition," Jade asked perking back up.

Erika took her up to the office where Ryan was already posted up watching the monitors.

"Anything interesting?" Erika asked.

"Just the stuff your freaky clients say," he replied laughing. "The guy with Cream wants her to dress like a man and Bree's client wants her to read freaky letters to him describing how he was a bad boy in class and needs to be spanked."

"That's mild compared to some of the things I've seen, but I will let you experience that for yourself. By the way this is my best friend, Jade. She just got in from LA."

"I noticed her car across the street, thought she was lost. Wow LA, must be really nice," Ryan replied making goo goo eyes at Jade. Saving Ryan from making a complete fool of himself, Erika told him to take a break.

Divine, White Chocolate, OhSoSexy, and Tasty were all in private shows by the time Jade and Erika were comfortable in the black leather office chairs. Divine looked like she was entertaining her TV more than her client while Tasty was doing her favorite, dominatrix. She was telling her client in a very commanding voice that he better not cum until she allows him to. White Chocolate was working out on her newly installed stripper pole so Erika decided to go with OhSoSexy. OhSoSexy was already down to nothing but her white thigh high stocking and clear stilettos by the time Erika and Jade clicked on the administrator voyeur view.

"You want me to ride you like a good cowgirl, baby?" OhSoSexy purred at her computer.

Yes, ride this dick baby! 9hard4u typed back. *Moan for me,* he quickly added.

OhSoSexy pulled out a stand alone dildo. She placed it on the floor and began to ride it like a champ. The dildo slid in and out of her with ease as she did squats on it.

"Mmmmmm, ooooh, aaah, this feels so good baby! You feel so good inside of me," she said in gasps.

Take it baby, take all of me! 9hard4u responded stroking his throbbing manhood faster and faster. He could feel his explosion building up inside of him like a volcano ready to erupt.

"Give it to me daddy!" she screamed.

Thank you baby, he typed disconnecting from the show.

"What the heck was that?" Jade said in between her laughter. "I mean he just cut her off."

"Girl please," Erika said rolling her eyes. "He came. That happens all the time they get what they want and end the show. She was lucky to get thanks. Sometimes they simply disconnect or run out of money before they get a chance to finish. She did great keeping him online and from cumming for 25 minutes with 4 other men sneaking a peak at the same time. She made $50 off the man who bought the private show and another $100 from the ones who voyeured in. Men like the voyeur option because it's cheaper. The girls like it cause they getting extra money off it. Of course my business percentage will be deducted, but hey she did not have to touch anyone or get her ass grabbed. And believe me OhSoSexy pulling out that dildo was all her idea. That girl is wild."

"Don't even remind me about guys grabbing or even touching me," Jade said kicking back in her chair. "I used to be so scared one of the men would get their cum on my body the way they were allowed to be butt ass naked at *Passionate Playmates*. I mean some of them would be whacking off, trying to aim at me as I played with myself, or danced over them. Not to mention some refused to shower and we know how bad that rotten cock smell was. Ewww!"

"I know. That was one of the main reasons I worked so hard to get the hell out of there. You think that show was a trip, let me show you Free Chat. Girl the broke men always try their best to see stuff for free!"

Erika scanned her monitors to see who was showing up in the top ten positions for the evening. Spice was number 2, right behind Asia, and the other new girl Amber was holding down the number 3 slot. The rest of the top ten had her usual girls. Some of whom Erika had noticed have gotten a little lazy, even in their private shows.

"You see how the men chat in different colors?" she said after clicking in Amber's room. "The men buy credits and how much is in their account dictate the different colors. Blue means they have $50 or more, yellow is $25 in up, green is $25 down to .50. And believe me they will hold onto that .50 just to show up in green. Last but not least is black font. Those are the men without credits and the main ones that be demanding the girls show something."

"I see," Jade said looking at a customer in black font trying his best to see some skin.

Show ass baby, Balling4life typed, *do it with your thongs off.*

In Private Chat, Amber typed instead of speaking out loud for fear that her voice would reflect how annoyed she was. Balling4life and many others had been trying to work her over for the past hour. She would have a private show and they would come back to her room as soon as she went back to Free Chat.

Show pussy and I will go private, promise.

Baby, that would be a little more believable if you at least had some credits. Now go get some or relax and enjoy the show, she responded before moving away from the keyboard so she could dance to her favorite song by Pink, *So What*, that was playing on yahoo music. The girls new full well not to believe the empty promises the men gave about going nude in Free Chat. Erika told them several times if someone wanted to go private they would. None of the *quid pro quo* crap ever worked. The girl would show her tits or ass for free, not get a show, and end up suspended from working a few days. It was not worth the risk.

*So what I'm still a rock star, I got my rock movies, and I will whoop you…tonight….*Pink's raspy voice belted out as Amber bounced her ass to the beat. She had not mastered the moves that Spice had from working at the strip club, but with practice she would soon give her a run for her money. Erika always peeked in on other girls shows to see how they were bringing in the customers, checking to see what worked the best.

Yes baby get me hard! another black font member typed.

I love your ass, Baller4life added with a smiley face pumping its heart next to it.

Do you do anal? the other member jumped back in.

*Incoming private show…*Amber heard the computer say before turning back around to the camera. Putting on a Colgate smile she got her mind right to rock her customers world, now that he was paying.

"Man, that's going to take some getting used to," Jade said taken back by some of the customers' vulgarity. "I'm used to getting paid before I hear all that."

"It is a bit different but you control the room. Most girls do very little of what the black font people say and encourage them to get credits. Funny, once that is said they back off. You also have the power to kick out the people who get on your nerves, or irritate the other customers in your room as well. They can come back but they have a whole new attitude and tend to even support you when other guys get out of hand asking for free stuff."

"I see and I also noticed that she didn't wait very long to get picked up for a show any way. I did see some guys were nice even though they were broke. They seemed happy just to see her beauty."

"Oh yeah, you can also clear the room by going to Nude Chat. Customers have to pay just to go in there with you because you can get as freaky as you want, and no black font can get in," Erika added before looking for another model's room to check out for Jade.

They watched several shows getting a good laugh off the perverted clients. Erika gave her a background on all the girls online and an update on her soon to be new club's progress. Jade filled her in on all the outrageous plastic surgeries the people in Hollywood, or whoever wanted to be famous, put themselves through just because someone didn't like the way they looked. The girls continued their reunion until the wee hours of the morning.

The next day Erika took Jade with her to check on the club's progression and to a meeting with the some of the models. Erika wanted to get a tally on who wanted to be in on her newest idea, a *Fantasy Girl* calendar; which she thought would be a great way of promoting her web site a little more. In Erika's business classes she learned to keep things fresh and always seek out new clientele. She was trying to reach the people who hadn't thought about logging onto the web in search of sexy women willing to please them and for those who used the web but didn't know about her site.

All the girls were excited about being in the calendar. Most saw it as an opportunity to be noticed and a chance to rub it in their old colleagues' faces about how well they were doing outside the strip clubs. The meeting was going fine until the girls started arguing when they tried to pick what month they wanted to be. Most of them wanted to be either June or December but others just wanted to be mean and vindictive.

"I want to be June," Diamond whined upset that two other girls beat her to it.

"June? You look more like October with all that makeup you have on," Pleasure interjected taking a moment to pause from filing her nails, "besides everyone knows that men need to have some Pleasure in the summertime."

"You have a lot of nerve to talk. You make all this money yet you still continue to go get those cheap ass kitchen hairdos and come out looking like a broke Beyonce," Diamond tossed back.

Containing her laughter Erika quickly squashed the issue. "I am the decision maker and some of you will be doubled up, in a group, or by yourself. You seem to forget there are other models in different states that need to be included," she said regaining control.

A few bitched and complained until Erika gave them the 'evil eye' letting them know she was not dealing with the diva syndrome. They wouldn't have to worry about sharing the spotlight. They wouldn't be in the calendar at all if they continued with this nonsense.

After getting the count of who all wanted to be in the calendar, which some didn't want to for personal reasons, like their boyfriend would be mad or they don't want to embarrass their parents, she sent an email from her cell phone to Kenny, with the list of names. When it came to the photo shoots Erika decided to let Kenny come up with the when, where, and how. He had an excellent eye for certain poses and did not want to be in his way. It was also away for her not to have to deal with all the attitude of the models trying to out shine one another for the spotlight.

"Now," Erika said closing her cell phone, "on to our next issue." Her tone silenced the entire room. She glanced around looking the girls over before continuing, "I know some of you have been on the site almost from the beginning and have built up a huge fan base, however your performances have been slacking. I noticed that some of you just sit at the computer and type the whole time in Free Chat even when the money customer ask to have a look at you. It is not hard for you to stand up, lean back, or hell pull your face away from your soap operas to show the customer your body. They aren't asking for much. Telling them to go private for everything is not the answer."

"Awww boss lady if they want us they will just go private," Diamond said breaking the silence looking at Erika with her arms crossed.

"Well," Erika said smiling because she knew Diamond would be the first to have a smart comment, "since you decided to speak up and let the room know that you were you are one of the culprits, lets talk about your last few shows. Shall we?" Erika reached into her Armani briefcase pulling out a stack of papers. "Let's see last night one of our gold members, as well as a member of your fan club asked you to stand up so he can see your outfit. Your response, 'in private'. Please explain why a gold member needed to pay to see your outfit? He was not asking for anything extreme. You know where he went? Right over to Spice's room and guess what? He asked her the same thing. She stood up, gave a little shake, and then spent a half hour in private with him. He even joined her fan club. To top it off, her doing the shake, caused a few others to voyeur in on the show."

"I mean, can't we have a bad day?" Diamond said trying to defend her actions.

"Bad day? Diamond you have been having a bad month. You are lucky he just didn't leave the site like some others have because of your attitude. Last week you told someone that they were interrupting your nap time. Nap time. Log off. I will do you a favor so you can get some sleep. As of this moment, you are on suspension for a week. Customers talk Diamond, and word of mouth is a killer. If those customers start talking about how rude you girls are that is bad for business, both for me and you. You have been getting by with your looks but that isn't enough. This is the sex industry and that is what sells honey not your face."

Diamond sunk back in her chair fuming. She had gotten so used to her regular customers dropping money on her left and right that she had gotten the big head and let it start to control her. Even more embarrassing was that a new girl got her show and she possibly lost out on one of her daily regulars.

"Ladies, yes you are all gorgeous but you have to give them something to want you to go private and to keep coming back. Yes, you may get a few who don't mind you sitting there and are willing to take a chance that you will do more 'in private', but do you really think they will keep coming back. This is business. Give them a little. Speaking of a little; it was not any of you here, but I have to say it again. Keep your freaking clothes on in Free Chat! None of this hand bra crap and letting a titty fall out. Why buy the cow when they are getting the milk for free?"

"Some of us just have extra sags," Pleasure said tossing a glance in Diamond's direction trying to get in an extra jab while she was down.

Holding up two fingers Erika gave Pleasure the signal letting her know she was inches away from getting in trouble herself before continuing, "As I was saying. No nudity, no sucking on toys, and definitely no masturbating in free chat. You want to do that then go to Nude Chat or wait for a freaking Private show. I have to fire someone for going to town on a dildo in Free Chat. I think it was so good to her that she forgot where the heck she was. She did not stop until she came and then when someone asked her to zoom in she had the nerve to reply in private. I swear I don't know what goes through some of you girls head."

"Boss Lady, you are lying no one really did that did they?" Spice said trying to contain her laughter by putting her hands over her mouth.

"I wish, but hey I am done rambling on for the day. Thank you for your time ladies and go make that money, don't let it make you." Erika really did wish it was a lie but that would be the fantasy. While showing Jade some shows she came across MsWorkIt shoving her toy all inside her. The only good thing is she actually logged off shortly after she had finished. The killer part is MsWorkIt had just come off of suspension for flashing her crotch. Erika reasoned that some girls just would not understand the business no matter how much she tried to teach them. She planned on terminating her later on that day.

Chapter 5

Erika sat silently on her blue and gold Ducati dreading walking into the Starbucks for her meeting with LaTisha, a.k.a. MsWorkIt. She knew exactly what needed to be done but LaTisha being a single mother of two was weighing heavy on her. LaTisha had been with *Fantasy Girls* a little over four months bringing in a fair amount of money for herself, so she hopped she was smart enough to save some of it.

Not wanting to prolong the inevitable Erika took off her helmet and changed out of her riding shoes into her newly purchased wedge heeled sandals. Smiling at the men who stopped to take notice, she headed towards the Starbucks entrance.

LaTisha worked for an insurance company when she first approached Erika about becoming a *Fantasy Girl*. Barely making it to her month marker, she turned in her two week notice to them. Erika tried to encourage her to work both, but LaTisha was grown and could do as she wished. In her monthly meetings she always tried to encourage her girls to have a back up plan because the adult industry did not come with a retirement package.

LaTisha patiently sat at one of the high round tables waiting for Erika to walk in the door. She was dressed business casual in a silk peach top, black slacks, and medium heels. Standing at 5ft 9in, she didn't want to wear anything over two inches and tower over people. She had her micro braids swept up into a bun on the side of her head so she could show of her 2k diamond earrings.

Walking up to the table, Erika took notice of how LaTisha's top matched her bronze eye shadow and lip gloss perfectly. Erika admired her flawless chocolate skin and size 9 body. LaTisha was thick in all the right places with a small waist, big hips, and D cup bra size. She reminded Erika of Tocarra Jones, the former *America's Next Top Model* contestant, now BET personality. This is was exactly why Erika hired her. Not all men want a size 2. A lot of them want to see someone that they felt was obtainable and LaTisha was that and more.

"You here to give me another lecture, Boss Lady?" Latisha asked taking a sip off her Root Beer.

"Not this time," Erika sighed taking a seat.

"Then what's up?" she responded getting nervous.

"Well since you been on the site you have been suspended for nudity in Free Chat a total of three times. What you did the other day was unacceptable. You were playing with a dildo for everyone to see. It may have been easier to take if you weren't shoving it all up inside you, and of course you were once again, nude. You know that Free Chat is not secure and children can be watching. Yes we have all the warning signs and you have to be a member to get in the site but still…" Erika said shaking her head.

"I thought I clicked the Nude Chat button," came her weak reply.

"Are you serious? You really expect me to believe that? You knew you weren't in Nude Chat when you saw the non paying customers still in the room. The only good point is at least you did make some money off of it because a few men decided to go cam to cam and show themselves stroking their penises, while you pleased yourself. The bottom line is you are too big of a risk to my business. You are a smart girl so I hope you have a backup plan. I am still confused by what would possess you to do that. Any way here is your final check," Erika finished. She handed LaTisha the check and headed for the door.

LaTisha took the check, placing it in her gold Dereon purse. All she could do was mumble a sincere apology to Erika's back. She was in shock. The guy told her they were testing the security of the site and Erika was fully aware. She knew she got a bit out of hand with her toy but never imagined she would get fired. Suspended a few days like always was what she had in mind. Gathering her belongings she headed towards her car.

Erika was relieved to have the burden off her chest. She put back on her riding shoes, hopped on her bike, and jumped on 38th St. heading downtown. It was a beautiful day out so she knew any and everyone would be hanging out. As she sped by she saw females walking down the street in their hoochie shorts, belly shirts, and high heels pushing their babies in strollers. Guys were rolling their pimped out rides with the 24 inch rims. The Muslims were on the corners selling their oils, incense, and bean pies. The rug man was out and even the man who rode a ten speed caring his radio seemed to be enjoying the day.

A guy she knew from the barber shop had his mobile car wash up and ready for business. He waved to her as he shined up an old school Cadillac with Gucci symbols painted on it. She chuckled to herself as she rounded the corner, turning left on Meridian.

By the time she made it downtown the traffic was bumper to bumper. Glad she chose to ride her bike, she averted traffic by going down alley's and in between cars. She made it to the spot where the riders hung out just in time to see Devon with two blonds, one black one white, on him trying to convince him to let them ride. The Sister was so bold she climbed on his bike straddling him. Her legs were spread so wide that her skirt was hiked up her legs allowing Erika to see the underwear that she wasn't wearing.

"What's up, Devon?" she said stopping her bike next to his and removing her helmet.

"Erika! My Girl!" he beamed while pushing No Panties off his bike. "She at least could have shaved that mess if she was going to let it all hang out like that."

"She was a hot mess. I bet your bike is funky now," Erika joked.

"Whatever, but I will spray it with Lysol just in case. How you been, Baby Girl? You talked to Kenny Lately?"

"I've been great. Business is good and Kenny is on a photo shoot with some of my girls."

"Photo shoot? Man, who knew that me hooking you two up would have him become a big shot photographer and you a big time business owner," he said getting back comfortable on his bike after wiping it off with hand sanitizer.

"Naw, we ain't big time. At least not yet, but one day who knows."

"How's my lil man doing? His daddy still up to his old tricks or is he locked up again for not paying child support?" he asked genuinely concerned.

"Shawn is fine and last I heard Sperm Donor was in his second home, jail. They picked him up for a suspended license, which of course was suspended because he is behind on child support. I only know because of course he called me collect like I care. I didn't answer, but I did call back to the courthouse to see what he was in for this time."

"No shit? What he think you were gonna bail him out?"

"If he did he is crazier than I thought. The money I make is not for him. He needs to get a job and quit living off of people. Enough about him, what have you been up too?" she said changing the sour topic.

"DJ'ing of course. Been doing real good at it too. Thinking about opening up a studio."

"Yeah, I have heard some of your mixes on the radio. Opening up a studio? I'm impressed. I may need to get with you later on to do some guest DJ'ing at my club when it opens," she said sliding in her new project.

"Club? Now I am impressed. I mean you talked about it but dang…I didn't know how serious you were. I honestly thought you were just a young girl with one too many dreams. Hell yeah I will do it. Whatever you need, Baby Girl. I gotta roll out but call me on the real. Don't be no stranger," he said looking at her in a new light. His little buddy was definitely something special.

She gave him a hug and watched as he rode off. The same two women that were messing with Devon noticed she was alone and started heading her way. "Oh hell no. You chics better kick rocks!" she shouted to them as she peeled off. There was no way in hell she was going to allow them to get on her baby.

***

"I don't care what other men say. There is no freaking way I could get turned on from some chic dancing when I'm sitting in a room with thirty other dudes," Xavier said trying to figure out why so many men just forked over their hard earned money to some female they didn't know.

He was sitting at the table with Erika helping her sort through what seemed like hundreds of pictures of her girls. Erika had received the calendar photos from Kenny earlier that day and she was trying to determine who she wanted on each month. She only asked him to help so she can get a different male perspective, on top of Kenny's favorites. From the way things were going, she would end up with two separate calendars.

"That's the point I'm trying to make, my site is one on one. No sharing. At least not with the clients' knowledge of when others are taking a peek. Most could care less any way because they are in the comforts of their own home," she argued while placing Asia's picture in her stack of favorites. Asia looked stunning in her red teddy lying on a white rug in front of a fire place. Now she knew what the judges were going through on *America's Next Top Model,* all the girls were beautiful but she wanted them top jump off the page at her.

"I've been to plenty of clubs, seen some fine and not so fine women. I am not gay but they just don't do it for me," he replied shaking his head.

"You are not getting the privacy or the connection," Erika said trying to get him to understand.

"Whatever, I don't care who it is or how private it is. I bet I won't even get hard."

"Oh really?" She snapped back twisting up her lips, looking at him like he was crazy.

"Every man isn't led by his other head, like you think. There are other things that motivate us."

"You want to bet?" she asked forming a plan to get her point across.

"Oh, I know where you're going. You just have to be right. I will take on whomever you send my way. Pull out your main girls if you want," he challenged throwing his hands up in the air.

"I won't be needed them," she replied with a sly grin. Grabbing Xavier by the hand she led him to the newly remodeled Players Lounge. She ushered him to the ottoman and left him sitting in silence.

Erika rushed back to her room grabbing one of her outfits. Instead of using the door from the hallway she entered through the bathroom door and snuck back in the room, behind the sheer curtain. Taking a deep breath she turned into her alter ego, Ecstasy.

"You ready for me baby?" Ecstasy said seductively.

"Show me what you got Ms. Lady," he replied clueless that Erika was the one in the room.

Pushing play on her iPod tower Ecstasy let the music get her in the mood, ready to blow Xavier's mind. She emerged from behind the curtain in a Leopard dress with a V neckline down to her navel barely covering her breast. It had slits on both sides coming all the way up to her waist showing her magnificently toned legs and black thong. Xavier sat up upright with his mouth wide open, then quickly composing himself he shrugged his shoulders and sat back on the ottoman.

Doing the classic stripper walk to the beat of Ciara's song Promise she walked with one leg in front of the other making her ass stick out farther than normal, working her way to the pole.

“The name is Ecstasy,” she purred facing the pole making sure to look him directly in the eyes before licking her lips and grabbing the pole with one hand. She walked around the pole slowly, then faster, to building up momentum in order to swing around the pole. She swung around letting her body flow freely with her head hanging back. As she came to a stop she placed her other hand on the pole. With the grace of a gymnast she wrapped her legs around the pole and let go of her hands. Now upside down she rolled her body, arching her back and stomach in deep waves, until she had moved all the way down to the floor. With her ass facing him she popped her back up and down to the rhythm of the music making her ass bounce at the same time. Sliding across the floor with her booty still bouncing she moved directly in front of him. Rising off her knees to a squatting position she laid her head back in his lap and stroked his thighs with her hands.

“Be still,” she whispered using her arms to do a backwards flip onto the ottoman landing with her legs around his with her crotch directly in front of his mouth. She did a few forward thrusts with her hips then slid down his body, back to the floor.

“Damn girl,” he murmured squirming in his seat.

“I’m just getting warmed up,” she replied standing in front of him with her legs slightly apart unlacing the strings of her dress. Once it was undone she let it fall to the floor. Bending over slowly she picked up the dress rubbing it across Xavier's body taunting him. Next she sat in his lap rotating her hips as if she was riding him, making sure he was hard as a rock. Stopping before he could climax she stood over him with one leg on each side of his body swinging her hips and playing with her breasts as she removed her black lace thong causing him to stare as if he were in a trance.

Ecstasy slid her hands down to her precious jewel fingering her bud until she was moist. Not able to withstand the torture any longer Xavier grabbed both of her butt cheeks pulling her down on his face and proceeded to slurp away.

Caught up in bliss, Ecstasy ground her hot body on his tongue while massaging his crotch with one of her feet. His penis grew until it was about to burst from the confinement of his jeans. Without missing a beat he slid his pants and boxers down far enough so he could kick them off the rest of the way. Grabbing her thighs he laid her down on the ottoman. Sucking her breasts he placed a condom on. Gently he slid in her juicy walls giving her what she had been waiting for. Pumping back with a fever of her own she matched his deep strokes. Changing positions Xavier moved behind her smacking her cheeks as he gave it to her doggy style. She could tell he was getting ready to cum when he grabbed her hips pumping faster.

"Ooooh, aaarggh," he said collapsing on top of her.

"I win," she whispered in his ear exhausted from all of her gymnastics.

Chapter 6

Normally Erika would have run a personal background check on someone she decided to be involved with, Xavier was special. It seemed as if she known him for years. He was so easy to talk to and he actually listened to what she had to say. They had become almost inseparable after the night she won the bet. They gave each other their space to handle their individual business; outside of that, they were always together. She had become so used to his company over the following weeks she started to include him in on her plans for the club. He even helped her get around the red tape downtown and obtain a liquor license.

Xavier surprised Erika with a gift to celebrate her progress, tickets for *The Color Purple* in New York starring Fantasia. He even went so far as to include Jade and her new found love, Ryan. Ryan had bugged her for two weeks straight to get Jades phone number. Erika told him to ask her himself but after seeing how nervous he was every time Jade was around she had mercy on him.

Everyone agreed that Oprah definitely was on to something turning the movie and book into a play. Erika thought Fantasia did a terrible job in her first acting role playing herself on *Lifetime* but did a complete comeback proving she was a true star in the play.

When Fantasia put that curse on ole Mr. the audience went crazy with a thunderous applause. Jade was still singing Sophia's *Hell No* song on the cab ride back to the hotel.

Taking an early flight back for a business meeting the next day, Xavier left the girls to enjoy themselves at the many stores before their flight later on that evening. They bought so many clothes, purses and shoes that they had to pay an extra $150 a piece for excess weight in their suitcases. All the shopping exhausted Erika, who slept the entire flight home.

Erika woke up the next morning feeling like the walking dead. "Oooh, my head hurts," she moaned searching her room for some Tylenol or Aspirin to take away the pain.

"Who the hell are you?" she said seeing her reflection in the mirror. The sight scared her, both eyes were blood shot red and her hair was a mess.

After they made it back in town from New York, Jade still wanted to party. It was Classic weekend so the clubs would be packed with any and everybody. A few 'B' list celebrities and Baller's were all supposed to be at Club Ice hanging out in the V.I.P. area. Jade was buddies with one of the DJ's at Hot 96.3. She called him up, securing their spot as soon as they touched the ground. They party was so live it resembled an R. Kelly video. The dance floor stayed packed and the folks who didn't dance rocked to the beat; waving their drinks in the air. They didn't leave the parking lot until well after 5:00am because they were hanging out running their mouths after the club had closed.

When her alarm went off she hit the snooze button four times before realizing she was supposed have a phone conference with a potential club investor. Reluctantly she got out the bed dragging herself to the shower, desperately trying to wake up. If coffee didn't upset her stomach she would have injected herself with it. As if on queue her business line was ringing as she stepped out the shower.

"Erika speaking," she said straining to sound chipper.

"Good morning! This is Edmond. I will get straight to the point. I love your business plan for the club. You have impeccable business sense and your vision can be a huge success with my help. I will be willing to front all of the money and you can just follow through with those brilliant ideas of yours," the person said talking non stop.

"Why thank you, but I don't need someone to pay for my business. I just need a small investment to put a credible name behind my project to bring in more white collar clientele, such as doctors, lawyers and CEO's," she responded now fully awake.

"That's exactly what I have in mind. You wouldn't have to worry about such thing, that's for me to do for you."

Not really having a good feeling about the investor, she politely ended the call telling him she had other people interested and she would get back to him. Even though she had no one else, Erika didn't want to risk of the Edmond trying to take over her dream. He was too high corporate for her. She was not going to be like so many other businesses in which a person has a vision, but not enough money, so they get an investor who lets the person with the idea get everything going and then the next thing they know the investor takes over, getting rid of the original person.

Instead of going back to sleep Erika watched a few early shows. Security wasn't due to arrive until 2:00pm when Asia was scheduled to work. She watched as Desire, a Latina goddess, put on a show imagining the man she was performing for was in the room with her. She was wearing a black sheer gown with a plunging neckline and feathers around the collar. Her bronze legs were straddled over a red velvet chair, with her head leaning to the side, letting her black wavy mane flow freely as she spoke seductively to her client in Spanish. Erika watched as Seduction moved her hands slowly across her breasts as if they were her client's hands exploring her body.

A movement in the corner of another entertainer's show caught her attention drawing her eyes away from Desire's private show. Amber, one of her newer girls, was putting on a performance that was sure to keep her client hungering for more. She was in the corner of her room doing a number on a sex toy that would put Heather Hunter to shame. Erika chuckled to herself while she watched as Amber's head bobbed up and down, her mouth engulfing the toy.

Erika's mouth fell open in disbelief when she realized Amber was not using a prop at all. There was a man in the room with her and she was performing on the real thing.

"Hell No! Not this crap! It is too early in the morning for this drama," Erika said to herself before pausing Amber's session and putting in a previously recorded show with a message apologizing for technical difficulties to tide the client over.

Erika sent Amber an instant message that read, 'be at my house within the hour, we need to talk now.' She could care less who she had in the room with her; the problem was Amber. She knew darn well what the rules were. Heck Erika covered them in her orientation with the rest of the paper work, requiring them to sign the bottom of the page. She was not running a porn site and refused to be placed in the same category.

No matter how hard she tried it seemed as if she was not getting through to the girls that they didn't have to screw someone to get paid. It may have been her boyfriend, but to Erika it made no difference. Now the client will think he can get full hardcore porn for the same amount as her other shows. Needing someone to talk to she started dialing Jade, hanging up before it even rang. She forgot Jade went over Ryan's when they left the club and would not answer the phone. She tried calling Xavier, his phone went directly to voice mail so she called Kenny.

Pacing the floor she asked, "Did you see that crap? See this is the mess I'm talking about. These heifa's always trying me!"

"I saw it and yes it was messed up. Now calm down so we can discuss what you want to do about the situation," he replied

"I want to kick her ass to the curb with a big dose of bitch be gone! What the heck do you think?"

"In other words you want to fire her?" he questioned trying his best to understand her shouting into the phone.

"Are you serious? I know you are from another country but please don't make me start translating this crap when I am upset because my anger will turn on you," she answered Kenny in a very controlled tone.

"I understood that 100% and I am taking her off the site as we speak," he said making sure he was not going to end up on the wrong side Erika's wrath. He knew first hand that when she was mad and the wrong person stepped in the way, she shredded them to pieces with her words.

Kenny agreed that she was not overreacting and it was a very wise decision to get rid of the girl. He felt if Erika was to give her another chance she will continue to push the envelope, besides Amber was not going to hurt the financial part of the business. She can get a girl to replace her just as fast as she hired her. Recently she had a few bored housewives wanting to show their sexy side.

Erika almost wore a hole in her carpet pacing the floor waiting for Amber. She just could not understand for the life of her why Amber would do such a stupid thing. She had been doing so well that Erika was sure she would be on Asia's level in a month or so. Hell, she recalled one particular show that turned her on and she was no where near interested in being with a woman.

Xavier and Keisha had just left after eating dinner and having a few cocktails but Erika was still too wired up to sleep. Going to her room, she flopped on her bed and turned her TV to the channel which allowed her to see the live shows directly from the bedroom. “The wonders of technology,” she said smirking. It’s not like she didn’t trust her security but she always liked to be hands on from time to time to see what the models were up to. She saw Amber had been live for almost 2 minutes so she decided to focus on her show to see what was causing her to be in the top five of her girls for the past few weeks.

Amber had her knees up on the couch slightly leaning over it dripping some sort of oil down her back, letting it run down her firm ass. Rubbing it in with her left hand, she produced a blue dolphin vibrator with spinning beads in the right. Looking at the camera she asked her client if he wanted her to suck it. Without waiting for a reply she began deep-throating it like her life depended on it making slurping sounds for a more heightened effect. When she was done she began moving the dolphin against her lower pink flower which was moist, ready, and waiting. She played with her clit using the spinning beads before giving into desire shoving the toy far up in her walls pumping in and out with vigorous thrusts as the dolphin's nose kept up the vibration on her clit. Her vaginal lips moving in and out in rhythm to the pumping motion caused Erika to squirm in her bed from the moisture forming in between her legs. The sounds Amber made were those of pure unadulterated passion. Not able to contain herself Erika slid her hand into her own panties fingering her own bud until she herself had exploded at the same time Amber hit her climax.

Calmed down with a glass of Italian wine in hand Erika was ready to handle the situation with Amber in a professional manner by the time she arrived. Kenny already had her removed from the site and Erika printed her final check. She was so glad she ordered a check making program for small businesses the month prior. This way she didn't have to wait for another company she had used in the past to process it. And it would have taken a week before they sent it back to her for her authorization. Call her paranoid but in this day and age she didn't trust anyone with her personal information.

If looks could kill Amber would have went up in smoke faster than a vampire getting caught by daylight. Even though Erika had on a poker face her eyes could easily give her away. Erika was more pissed off when Amber opened up her mouth.

"Is there something wrong?" she asked with her sweat outfit on, no make-up, and her hair in a pony tail looking like an innocent school girl appearing to be oblivious to what she had done.

Erika didn't blink; she could play the game just as well. She was not about to be manipulated by an amateur nor was she about to sit and go step by step over Amber actions. Doing so would give her a chance to plead her case trying to sway Erika's opinion on if it was wrong or not.

"You are aware of the rules, right?" Erika said pointing for Amber to have a seat in the exact same spot where she conducted her first interview.

"Yes, but I thought…"

"You thought wrong," Erika said cutting her off in mid sentence, "here is your check and you have been removed from my site. You just told me you were aware of the rules so there was absolutely no confusion. So in the words of Donald Trump you're FIRED!"

"Whatever! We will see who gets the last laugh," she spat back snatching her check from Erika's hand so hard she almost ripped it in half.

Ignoring her last statement Erika held open the door for Amber to exit.

"I wish you well. I hope you find something else you're good at," Erika replied in a fake extra bubbly voice.

"Piss off," Amber said brushing past her trying to slam the door on her way out but Erika had a tight grip on it.

"Just keep on giving me more reasons to let you stay," Erika retorted sarcastically, shutting the door in her face.

It took everything Erika had not to snatch Amber bald. Having a business to run she could not get caught up in a cat fight. Erika came out on top without throwing a punch anyway. People behaving like Amber got on her last nerves. They do something wrong and get mad at the repercussions for their actions like they are the victim.

Pushing the buttons on her cell, Erika tried calling Xavier again.

"What's up boo? I just got out of a meeting. You sound upset. What's the matter?"

"Amber had someone in the room with her giving them a blow job while in one of her shows."

"What? That is wild. I'm about 15 minutes from your house. I'm on my way."

"Well you better get here quick before I change my mind about kicking her ass and go after her."

"Hold on, Erika, no need to turn into the *Terminator* on the girl. I will get there as fast as I can," Xavier replied picking up speed in his truck. He hadn't seen Erika's anger first hand, but he had heard about her beating the crap out of some chic she used to work with. Jade told him how another model got a beating of her life for making a racist comment to Erika, Foxy, and another model. At shift change they took the girl on a ride in Foxy's suburban, and each girl took their turn kicking the model's butt. He could imagine Erika clear as day pulling up to Amber at a stoplight, opening up the poor girl's car door and dragging her to the street.

"I promise I will stay put until you get here," she huffed.

When he arrived, she gave him the run down on everything that happened with Amber before he made it all the way into the living room. She explained how she fired her and how she had to refrain from knocking her upside the head.

"Did you see who was in the room with her?"

"I didn't care," she replied. "She knew damn well what the rules were, she signed the contract, and she is the one I fired! She is so lucky Jade wasn't here. We would wait until its dark and go beat the crap out of her. I keep a black sweat outfit in my car just for silly crap like this."

"Dang woman, calm down. You went from being the *Terminator* to Batman without Robin. Relax, release, relate or something just don't bite my head off."

"My bad," she laughed. "I am just mad at the world right now. I really am more upset at myself. I broke my own rules from the start when I hired her in the first place.

She has a lot of potential, but if I let this crap slide then everyone else will be trying some B.S. I saw how that mess went down first hand when I was working at the club. Those girls will try to throw it back in my face if I tried to get on their case about anything if I let this go. And I don't need any more drama. She better be lucky I am a business woman and am tired of using my hands to solve all my problems. I'll just pay some crack head to get her."

"Shut up. You are killing me. You no dang well you aren't paying anyone to do anything. I understand you have a right to be mad and I would too. Now come here so your man can work out your tension," he said giving her the knowing look that lovers share.

"You so nasty," she smiled walking towards him.

"Naw, you are. Get you're mind out the gutter. I was talking about a massage you freak," he replied innocently placing his hands on her shoulders when she sat in the chair in front of him. "But if that's what you want to do…"

"I can't believe you. You just said I had my mind in the gutter. Whatever boy, shut up and give me a massage and you might get some loving after I finish handling my business this afternoon Mr."

Chapter 7

Heather could not believe the sight in front of her, Ecstasy was on the front of a calendar with Jade and some other girls promoting her web site. Just looking at Ecstasy made Heather want to throw up. Here she was being used and abused while Ecstasy and Jade were living it up. She stared at the picture of them smiling, wondering what the heck she ever did to deserve this life.

"What you looking at Heather?" Nitasha a Russian beauty said. "You know those girls?"

"In another life," Heather mumbled. "I'll take a pack of Newport's." The gas attendant slid the cigarettes to her and she handed him $5 off the measly $20 that she was allowed to have.

"Those sure are some sexy mamas'," the attendant said whistling, looking at the calendar, "I would give them my whole paycheck."

"What the hell are we? Chop liver?" Nitasha asked.

"Believe me your small check couldn't afford what they are selling," added Heather putting a smoke up to her mouth and lighting it. "Come on so we can get back. I don't feel like getting my ass kicked today."

"And I don't feel like putting my mouth on some wrinkled old dick either," Nitasha replied taking a long drag off the cigarette as if it were a magical potion to cure all of her problems.

The girls headed back to the hotel before someone was sent after them. They were only allowed ten minutes to run to the gas station on the corner. No excuses. If the line was too long then you just better drop what ever you were about to purchase and run like a bat out of hell back to the hotel before your time was up. If another customer wanted to speak to you; your only response should be trying to get him back to the hotel.

Heather and Nitasha got along better than the rest of the girls. They had an understanding. They were both stuck in the same situation so why make it any worse than they needed to by fighting with each other. She couldn't say that for the other prostitute who assaulted them with a million questions when they entered in the lobby.

"What took you so long?" Victoria asked popping her gum.

Nitasha shot back a smart remark, "Heather was having fantasies about becoming a calendar girl."

"In her dreams, she's just another ho like the rest of us."

"Whatever, Victoria. You are too stupid to know any better," Heather said taking her place in the lobby to catch a customer's eye.

It was hard for Heather to understand how these men could just walk in and pick one of them to have sex, pay his money, and leave like this crap was normal. What woman in her right mind would want to stand around waiting for some stranger to come and bang her head up against the headboard? On the other hand it wasn't like they really looked like the typical prostitute either. They were dressed in normal every day clothes and kind of blended in with the rest of the hotel guests. They even had their own section of the hotel that they took their Johns to.

The entire setup was something right out of a porno. A guy can be at the bar, one of the girls would go over to him, whisper something in his ear and they would be up in a room going at it like rabbits in less than two minutes. Whatever the case may be Heather was sure she was close to having enough money saved to get away without getting caught. She found out that her sister had gotten the better end of the deal. She started having panic attacks after her first experience. Not being able to work despite being beat;

their captives dropped her of at a mental hospital. Heather had made contact with the hospital preparing to have her sister released when she was ready to make her escape.

A few more weeks and she would be free. She overheard her Pimp discussing going out of town to pick up some more girls. While he was gone she was going to make a desperate attempt to get away. Heather didn't include anyone on her plans not even Nitasha. The risk was too great to take any chances.

***

If Erika wasn't scared she would break her neck, she would have done a back flip when she added up the total sales from stores buying her calendars. Grocery stores put them in their magazine and book isles, adult stores put them up front next to their *Vivid Girls Calendars,* book stores, gas stations and mini marts even had them.

"Are you still celebrating?" Xavier asked coming up behind her kissing Erika on the neck.

"Shouldn't I be?" Erika asked. "I feel like I am at the top of my game right now. I have a successful business in less than a years time, I am about to open up a bar, and I have a sexy man who isn't intimidated by me."

"No, you have every right. By all means continue. I would love continuing to watch you dance around the house but we are going to be late for your meeting with the contractor if you keep it up."

"It's after 2 o'clock already? Give me a few minutes to grab my jacket and put on my boots and we can be on our way," she said rushing out the room.

It took Erika less than three minutes to whip her hair up into a bun so she could look more professional, put on her cream suit jacket, Jimmy Choo spiked boots, and a dash of lip gloss on her lips before returning to her living room where she had left Xavier standing.

"You just blew the theory of a woman taking forever to get ready out the water," he said smiling at her quick change.

"Many years of fighting with four other siblings for one restroom," she replied doing a classic runway model turn showing off her new look.

Xavier's skillful driving got them through I70 traffic and to their destination in record time. Finding a parking space was another issue. The lot next to her building was full from all the people working in the downtown corporate offices. After circling the block a few times he gave up and pulled in a parking garage around the corner.

Erika assumed Shayla would be standing outside looking at her watch; keeping time like a hall monitor by the time they arrived. Shayla was only allowed to be there as a friend. The job had ended when the sale was complete, so she would just have to get over it. To their surprise Shayla actually showed up a few seconds after she and Xavier walked in the building. She claimed that parking had been an issue for her as well.

"So what do think?" Erika asked looking at Shayla and Xavier waiting for their opinion on the private rooms the contractor added to her building. The contractor took a large space upstairs, sectioned it off into three rooms, and did the same to an open area on the main floor. The new editions fit in so well, they seemed to have been there the entire time.

"Very nice," Shayla replied giving her the thumbs up.

"I'm impressed. But explain it to me again. This isn't a strip club but if a gentleman or, even a woman wanted some entertainment they can pay to go to one of the rooms for a personal show," Xavier said.

"That's it in a nut shell. The best of both worlds; they can mingle with people in an upscale club setting and for a little extra they can get their fantasy fulfilled in the back. If sex is in their fantasy then they came to the wrong place."

"Are you going to have men entertainers too?" Shayla wanted to know.

"Not at first only because I don't have any male employees, but hey you never know what the future holds,"

Erika assured her. "Now let's get out of their way so the construction crew can finish cleaning up."

"Excuse me Ms. Johnston, before you leave I just wanted you to know that some plumbing issues came up in your office. I went ahead and installed a shower instead of leaving the maintenance sinks in it. I hope it was okay," Steve said.

The contractors all worked for Steve who was a very young entrepreneur. He started out as an apprentice while in high school, continued working through college, starting his own company the day after he graduated. He was doing very well for himself.

"A shower? That didn't even cross my mind. That is a very good idea. Glad you took the initiative and installed it before telling me about it."

"I had a feeling you would like it. Have a nice day," he said looking her in the eyes instead of in her C cups as he did on their first encounter. Erika was used to men's roaming eyes so she let it slide as long as he was able to control himself when it was time for business. Once she started explaining what it was she wanted Steve became very professional and has not slipped since then.

Having a house to show, Shayla went her own way when they left the building. Erika rode with Xavier back to her house. Erika was still hyped off the progress of the club talking a mile a minute only stopping to take a breath of air.

"You're not coming in?" Erika questioned Xavier when he pulled up in her driveway but didn't turn off the car.

"I have a meeting with a potential client in less than an hour and I need to grab my briefcase from my condo. I will be back in time for some of you're mouth watering stuffed pasta shells," he said giving her a peck on the lips before she closed the door to his truck.

Not even Xavier missing her cooking could stop her joy. He ended up calling saying the meeting was taking longer than expected. If she wanted she was more than welcome to go to his Condo and wait for him because he would be too tired to drive across town to her house after the meeting.

If Erika was going to drive to his house and wait then she was going to make it a special evening for the both of them. She packed up some of her sexy lingerie, bubble bath, and massage oils to take with her. She was almost out the door when her home phone rang.

"Erika Johnston?"

"Yes."

"Ma'am this is the police department and we were called to a building you own. There seems to have been a bit of vandalism. We need you to come to the scene as soon as possible."

“Vandalism, are you serious? What did they mess up?”

“We don’t like discussing these things over the phone you need to come downtown please.”

Knowing Xavier wouldn’t answer his phone if he was in the middle of negotiations so, she called Kenny. He sounded half asleep when he answered the phone. After catching him up on what the officer told her he agreed to meet her at the building.

Chapter 8

Wiping the thick white substance off the side of her mouth as she grabbed the crumbled up money off the nightstand, Heather walked into the restroom locking the door. Standing on the edge of the tub she pushed up the ceiling tile in search of a small purple Crown Royal bag she had hidden up there. Not feeling the bag right away almost caused her heart to stop; then finally, her fingertips brushed against the string and she yanked it down.

Rushing to put her jeans back on and gargle with the tiny Listerine bottle from the hotel basket on the sink she yelled to her John that she would be out in a second. When she came out of the restroom he was sitting on the edge of the bed with an impatient look on his face.

"Some nerve. He can have sex with me and cum on my face but he can't wait for me to get cleaned up, asshole," she mumbled under her breath before speaking loud enough for him to hear. "You ready, honey?"

Saying nothing in return he followed her out into the hallway picking up his pace to get in front of her, he quickly exited the hotel.

"I'm going to the store," she said walking out the revolving door before any of the other girls had a chance to respond.

The city bus was pulling up to the corner just as she had anticipated when she made it to the front of the store; which was out of site of the hotel. Without a second thought she stepped on the bus ducking down in a seat just in case someone was coming around the corner.

With her heart racing she said a silent prayer to herself and calmed herself down. After she was positive the bus was out of eyesight, she allowed herself to relax in the seat.

Thirty minutes later the doors from the city bus closed behind her leaving Heather a block away from the Grey Hound station. Sprinting to the ticket booth she made it in just enough time to purchase a ticket before the bus pulled off. On one of the bus breaks she bought a prepaid cell phone from a Ma and Pop gas station and called her family letting them know she was on her way home.

Heather rode the bus until she reached Phoenix, Arizona and then took a cab to the airport. While she waited for the cab she went into a Burger King bathroom, putting on a brunette wig she purchased when she bought the cell phone. A day prior Heather had slipped the wallet out the purse of a dark haired woman sitting at the bar having a drink. When the lady was preoccupied with the bartender she removed her license and slipped the wallet back in her purse without detection.

With the stolen identification she bought a plane ticket and was on her way to Indiana within the hour. As the plane taxied on the runway for take-off she placed a call to the mental hospital to confirm the transfer of her sister to be closer to her family.

***

"What the hell do you mean someone came in busted the pipes!" Erika said pacing the room careful to avoid the side of the room with the water damage.

"Ms. Johnston, brand new pipes rarely burst on their own with no water running," Steve said trying to reassure her that the damage was not caused from negligence on his part. "I installed the plumbing in the whole building better than what the code says."

"Erika, listen to the man. Do pipes bursting throughout the whole building make sense to you?" Kenny said pleading with her to back off the contractor.

"Then what is he doing here?" she countered.

"I left some of my tools that I needed for another job."

"Mighty convenient," she snapped.

"Ma'am your contractor is the one who called the police so why would he be the one to damage it. If you think he did this on purpose then you have been watching too many crime shows," the partner of the officer who called Erika said halting the accusations.

"I don't, not really any way. I just can't understand why someone would break in and destroy a place that isn't even in business yet," she answered dumbfounded at the sight in front of her.

"Ma'am you would be surprised at the things kids do these days. We are pretty sure that's who it was because nothing was taken. You seem to have cameras all over the place and several computers in an office upstairs. If you don't mind me asking, what are they for?"

"Sir," Kenny interrupted, "can you please focus on the matter at hand. If you must know the cameras are for security. We did not think to activate it yet because the club was not open."

"Understandable, here is your case number," the older of the pair said handing her a business card before getting in their patrol car, "we will call you if we find out anything."

"You'll call? What type of crap is that?"

"Let it go. They really don't have anything to go on right now. Let them do their job," Kenny said stopping Erika from following the police to their car.

"That's some crap and you know it! Steve, how long is it going to take to fix this?"

"I know you don't want to hear it but at least six weeks. The water destroyed the drywall and carpet everywhere it was able to reach."

"Six weeks," she replied in a whisper.

"Sorry, but it's the best I can do. I will have my guys get on it first thing in the morning."

Not trusting Erika's state of mind Kenny followed her to make sure she made it home safely. Once her garage door made contact with the ground he pulled off.

Walking directly to her room she collapsed across her bed fully clothed.

"What," Erika said answering her cell phone. Looking at her alarm clock she realized two ours had passed.

"Where you at? I was expecting to come home to you laying butt naked on my bed," Xavier said joking.

"At home. I had a ruff night. Someone vandalized the club."

"What? I'm on my way and then you can tell me all about it," he said disconnecting the call.

Erika did not get a chance to tell Xavier what happened until the morning. When he arrived he carried her back to her room making her terrible night a little more bearable. He treated her the way all women deserve to be treated. He sucked and licked her from head to toe, making sure he took his time to explore every inch of her luscious body. By the time he was finished she could have cared less if someone came and set her bed on fire to care about the vandalism at her club.

Xavier relaxed her enough to keep her mind occupied while she was awake but sleeping was another issue. Erika tossed and turned before drifting off to a fitful night of non-rest. She kept having dreams of faceless teenagers breaking into her club while she was in it, but she was unable catch them.

"Sleepy head," Xavier said shaking Erika's arm. "Wake up, I have to go but Kenny filled me in on the incident while you were sleep. It's almost noon. You being the busy body you are, I know you have a full day so get up."

Yawning she said, "You're right I do have a few errands to run before Shawn gets home. Oh my god, I forgot to take him to school."

"Don't worry I told him you needed to rest and took him. He made it on time. Hey, this is just a minor set back don't let it get you down, okay," Xavier said staring deep into her brown eyes.

"Okay, I'm up now. I will focus on making the damage work for me some how," she responded giving him a half smile.

"That's my girl. Now, you do remember I have to go to Chicago to set up my guys with a new client. I will see you in a few days. Sorry I have to leave with things like this but I can't risk losing this client."

Understanding Xavier was the owner of his own company and was trying to make a name for himself just as she was trying to do with *Fantasy Girls*, Erika reluctantly got up walking him to the door.

Bzzzz, bzzzzzzz Erika's cell phone was vibrating on her nightstand as she was getting dressed.

"Speak to me."

"I heard you've been having some bad luck lately," the person on the other end spoke in a vaguely familiar voice.

"Who is this?"

"Has it been that long Ecstasy? You are a big bad business woman and now you don't know me," the person replied with boldness.

"Heather, is this you?"

"Oh, so now you no longer have amnesia? We need to meet and talk," Heather said.

"Talk? You're in town? When did you get here?"

"Like you care," Heather said cutting her off. "Meet me in the food court of the Circle Center Mall in an hour."

"An hour? What the heck makes you think you can come making demands of me? You have the nerve to come to me with an attitude when I have done nothing to you and you think I'm am about to meet you any where," Erika said. She had no clue what Heather's problem was but she had her own issues to deal with today.

"Oh, so you scared," Heather challenged.

"Scared of who, you? Whatever, you must really be high to talk to me like that. I'm not scared and I won't be tricked into coming. As a matter of fact I'm about to hang up. Don't bother calling me back," she laughed at Heather, hanging up in her face.

Erika felt as if her world was falling apart right before her eyes. She needed the club in order to prove herself as a legit business woman. The online business was doing better than she ever imagined but she yearned for more. She wanted to have a back up in case her online business fizzled out one day. *Never put all your eggs in one basket*, whoever said that knew exactly what they were talking about. Actors and Music Entertainers lived by that motto on a daily basis. They would have acting, singing, producing, managing and even writing all under their belt to keep themselves well rounded and so would she.

Bzzzz, bzzzzz her phone vibrated again. Picking up her cell she saw Private Call on the display.

"Yes," she said praying it wasn't Heather again.

"Miss Johnston, this is Edmond, did you I catch you at a bad time? I truly hope not because I was hoping you thought about my offer and have reconsidered my company as an investor."

"No, I have not," she stated firmly. "I told you I have chosen someone else."

"Well whatever they are offering I will double."

After her present bad luck she was tempted but her instincts would not allow her to be swayed by more money.

"Sorry, I am quite sure someone else would love your offer. Now if you'll excuse me I was in the middle of something very important."

Irritated by her bothersome phone calls she refocused her attention on her business plans to open her club in two months. She decided to place a call to a number for an interior decorator she had written down from a magazine she had read while at the dentist office. To her luck the company was able to have someone available that afternoon.

Kenny was going to be a co-owner in her club therefore she needed to include him on most of the decision making. His phone rang six times before going to voicemail. Leaving him a detailed message she snapped her phone shut. Lately it seemed that Kenny had been ignoring her calls unless it was for business purposes. She had the faintest idea as to why but was not going to ask him either. If he wanted to act like a spoiled brat then that was his problem not hers.

Much to her surprise, because he did not return her phone call, Kenny met Erika at the company's store located at Keystone at the Crossing. There was several design books placed on the table along with pieces of fabric. After looking over some of the books they came up with and the idea of an upscale elegance design. She would turn the upper level into a fine dinning Bistro which would double as her VIP area overlooking the main floor of the club. The look would bring in more of the corporate crowd but not overwhelm the blue collar worker if they chose to stop by.

This club had nothing to do with Erika's love of the Hip Hop world, she was just not going to allow herself to be limited. So many of those clubs start out well and then slowly meet their demise to fights and shootings. She planned on having a few Hip Hop concerts here and there but not so many that it would turn into a thug haven. She would also incorporate Jazz, Blues, Alternative, and R&B to round out her clientele. Erika dreamed of her club being as well known as those in LA, New York, and Atlanta. When people came to town, her club would be the place to be.

"So are you going to tell me the name of the club today Miss Lady?" Kenny asked on the elevator ride down.

"*Club Secrets*, what do you think?"

"With your private dance rooms, I think that is the perfect name," he replied smiling.

"Glad you like it," she answered. Now that she had him talking she was tempted to ask why he had been so distant lately but decided against it.

"You know I love all of your ideas. I keep telling you that you are a very smart lady," he stated very genuine.

"So you keep telling me."

"So, ummm, are you and Xavier pretty serious?" Kenny questioned uncomfortably.

"Serious as in we're making wedding plans, no. But I do enjoy his company. He seems to really understand me and we have a lot in common."

"Just don't fall in love too fast, okay. Looks are not everything and I know his type."

"Are you serious? Is this the reason you haven't been answering my calls? You are jealous," Erika responded finally discovering the reason for Kenny's distance.

"Forget I said anything, Erika," he said in a huff. Stepping off the elevator he made his way to his car in a pace so fast she couldn't have kept up if she tried.

She watched as he got farther and farther down the street finally disappearing before she turned heading in the direction of her car. Erika hit the highway back to her side of town with lightning speed. She had to get her son's daycare before they closed. Keisha had to work late at the law firm, working on a court brief, and would not be able to get him for her. Erika thought it was silly that the daycare closed at 5:30 instead of 6:00 like the other's in the arca, but after doing extensive research this one was the best.

After giving the daycare owner another hefty check for the month, she put Shawn in his booster seat, continuing on their way home. When Shawn was content from eating dinner and playing on his V-tech Pedal & Learn game she headed downstairs to go handle business. She had a stack of applications for women trying to join *Fantasy Girls* and for her private rooms at the club. Some of the girls were cute but not sexy enough to be a *Fantasy Girl,* ended up in a separate stack to be sorted through later. Instead of giving them a flat out no, she may extend an offer to be a hostess at her new club.

"Uh, Boss Lady," Ryan said getting her attention. "You have a dude at your front door looking kind of suspicious. I went to check him out and he claims to be your baby daddy."

"You got to be kidding me. What the heck does he want now? I haven't seen or heard from him in months."

"You want me to get rid of him?"

"No. I can handle him, thanks." Erika said slipping into her house shoes heading towards the front door.

"Can I help you?" Erika said leaving him no room to doubt she had an attitude.

Looking her up and down while licking his lips he said, "Yeah, I want my son."

"Do I smell alcohol? Are you drunk?" Erika snapped noticing how glazed his eyes were.

"No. I mean, I uh had a few drinks but you know me. I ain't drunk," he said with a smile trying to put his charm on her that had long since worn off.

"No I don't know you. If I did I would know where you have been for the past six months. I know you got out of jail and haven't heard a peep from you, not even asking about your son. And now you think you can come over to my house demanding things. You can get him on the weekend like you are supposed to. Today is Tuesday, come back sober on Friday."

"Whatever," he said dismissing her comment. "Why you still got me paying child support when you living large anyway? You know I can barely find work," he finished, while trying to look past her to get a better view of the inside of her house. He hated how she never let him in. All he wanted to do was see how nice the place was.

"And who fault is that? You stay sober, you might keep a job and the child support is for your son. Not me. That little $57 a week can't pay for nothing in my house. I put Shawn's money in a savings account for him."

"Really?" he said. Erika could see the wheels spinning in his head. "Can I have some?"

She hated the way he stood there looking at her rubbing the hairs on his goatee as if he just hit the jackpot. "No, you didn't! The money is for your son, not for you or me. Look, D'wayne, if you really want him, come back on Friday."

Erika quickly closed the door leaving him standing alone on her front porch. D'wayne stomped off to his dented Ford Escort, mad at the world. He bought the old beater with the intent of getting it fixed up a few months prior, but seemed to never have enough money. He started to slap her for those smart remarks but then he remembered the jail time he got for the last time he hit her, not to mention the big dude who answered the door. D'wayne wondered who the heck did that dude think he was any way.

"I told you she wasn't going to let me get him," he told his new live-in girlfriend. He had been trying to impress her by lying about how he had to beg and plead with Erika to see him and she never did. He purposely came by on a weekday without calling cause he knew Erika would say no. He knew Erika would stick to the child support order and if it had been the weekend she would have handed him over. He made that mistake two years ago when he came by on a Friday pretending his car had broken down he parked around the corner. He was hoping to just spend an hour with Shawn because he planned to go out. Erika messed that all up by packing Shawn up and giving him bus fair. He should have been thankful Erika never bugged him about Shawn.

"Damn, her crib is nice!" his girlfriend said interrupting his thoughts.

"Yeah, whatever," he mumbled before peeling out leaving black marks on the ground where he was parked.

Chapter 9

Xavier sat across the table from the mid aged lady who was once a very beautiful young woman and chatted away. There were a lot of people outside enjoying the sunshine with them.

"So I see she has fallen for you," the lady said taking a long drag on her cigarette. She was careful not to blow out the smoke in the direction of a little girl walking past.

"Yes she has, but she does keep her guard up."

"Don't worry you are very charming. I am sure she will totally give in to you
soon enough. How is this club business of hers coming along? I will give her credit she is a persistent one."

"That she is. Speaking our time is almost up, and I have to run. I was supposed to meet up with Erika 45 minutes ago." He leaned into her kissing her on the forehead before standing to leave.

"You know I love you, right?"

"But of course," she said with sadness. She hated when he had to leave her.

***

Erika sat in her burnt orange lazy boy in her den letting her mind wander. With one leg propped up on the right arm of the chair, she let the other foot dangle, barely keeping her purple fuzzy slipper on her toes. Anyone walking in the room would more than likely assume she was sleep because her eyes were closed. She sat silently analyzing the recent events trying to figure out if there was something she missed. The vandalism at the club, Kenny's odd behavior, the investor hounding her, baby daddy drama, and Heather showing back up were giving her a migraine.

She wasn't buying what the police were trying to sell her about a bunch of kids busting some pipes yet ignoring the computers sitting there for the taking. They may have not been smart enough to sell them, but they were smart enough to take them for home usage. If someone tried to break in again they would have to deal with her Brinks alarm system and two Dobermans, one of her friends had gladly given her. She even had Kenny turn the camera's on so she could spot the culprits red handed.

Kenny's behavior, however silly it was, finally had reasoning behind it. He was jealous of her and Xavier blooming relationship; which made absolutely no sense to Erika. Kenny wanted a woman who was way more reserved than she would ever be. He made it perfectly clear on their first photo shoot in the Bahamas, when she was just getting her business started, that he was not a play toy when she was merely dancing with him.

Erika knew she would be able to handle the investor and keep him at bay and D'wayne was harmless; nerve wrecking, but harmless. He showed up ranting and raving pulling a stunt like this once a year it seemed like.

Heather coming back to town was a whole other issue. She knew something was up with her when she looked on the Bunny Ranch website and didn't see a picture or her name among the rest of the girls. She didn't know what Heather was really up too, but what ever it was it changed her from the girl she used to be. She was used to Heather being extremely passive; much unlike the person she had spoken to on the phone. Heather was confident, aggressive and almost threatening. They were never truly close but it was no reason for Heather to now see her as the enemy.

When Erika was little her mother always told her that people who had money always had more problems because other people wanted to take what they had. They felt the person did not deserve their good fortune. It did not matter if the individual had worked for everything they had people would find something negative to say.

“Mama, why those girls always pick on me?” a fifteen year old Erika asked her mother after two bigger girls had teased her about being too skinny at school.

“They are just jealous baby. They want what you have. You have lots of friends, you don’t just play sports you dominate everything you attempt, and you are cute,” Mama Johnston answered her daughter as she caressed her hair.

“So it has nothing to do with these two mosquito bites on my chest that are supposed to be breasts,” she asked with tears ready to spill over her eyelids.

“Mosquito bites? Is that what they said? Let me tell you something you are my daughter and regardless of the size of your chest you will be someone and those girls know it. They tease you because they want to be you and because they can’t they try to destroy you, but honey you are my child and Gods creation. There is nothing they can do to you to stop you from being who you are destined to be.”

Erika smiled thinking of her mother. She always had a way of setting things right and never judging her. Mama Johnston didn’t even blink when Erika first mentioned she was dancing in a club. Now that she owned her own site her mother was even more supportive. She always said if you are going bother to do anything to be the best at it.

Now that she was on top she reasoned it was about time for people to try and pull her down. Well she wasn't going down without a fight. She will come out on top no matter what, she worked too dang hard to get were she was. She refused to go back to working temporary agencies, letting her pretty blue and white diploma from Indiana State University collect dust.

A few months earlier she got a good laugh at the expense of one of the girls who used to taunt her back in high school. Alexis sent Erika a message to her *Facebook* page asking if she remembered her. How could she forget, Alexis and her crew chased her home on more than one occasion. Erika could fight head up, but against a group of girls she was no fool. She started to say no but was curious to see how the girl was living and accepted her friend request. Come to find out the once curvaceous Alexis was now the obese Alexis, had four kids by four different men, and was working part time at some call center making no more than $10 an hour. Karma was a bitch.

"Somebody's got to be on top so it might as well be me," Erika sighed.

"Ma," Shawn walked in the room interrupting her thoughts, "can you read this book to me?"

Placing the book, *Little Nikita,* in her hands he pulled her from the chair to the couch so he could sit next to her. He was too big to climb in her lap but it didn't stop him from snuggling up close to her eagerly waiting for his mom to start reading.

"Little Nikita was a young boy living in Africa…." Erika read. She always made sure she read to him on a regular basis even though he was learning to read himself. It was her way of bonding with him. The books she bought always had people of different nationalities in them. When he asked her why one day she replied that was the way the world is.

Erika read to him until he started nodding off. When he was all the way sleep she carried him upstairs to his bedroom. Pulling his Spiderman covers over him she kissed him on his cheek and turned out the light.

Back in her den she pulled out a pad of paper, writing up an article for her new *Fantasy Girl* of the week. Realizing a week had almost past after her strained conversation with Heather she was no longer able to focus on what she was doing. Erika made a decision to end the nonsense. Pulling out her cell she decided to call her up and see what her problem was.

"Oh, so now I am supposed to jump because Ecstasy commands it?" Heathers said smacking on a piece of gum.

"Look, you are the one who wanted to meet with me. I have some free time so where can we meet?" Erika replied. She was already regretting making the call.

"Okay, spoiled brat, lets meet in two hours in the same spot as I said before."

"Fine." Hearing no response Erika glanced at her phone seeing call ended on the display.

Erika refused to let Heather's attitude and being constantly hung up on get under her skin even though it was easier said than done. Two hours was perfect enough time for Erika, it gave her enough time whip up a quick meal and drop Shawn off at her sister's. Not one to be caught in a trap she called up Jade for backup. She was far from scared but the way Heather was acting she wasn't taking any chances being caught off guard by a lunatic drug addict.

Packing up some food for Keisha as a piece offering for her watching Shawn on a short notice, Erika headed out the door. Picking up Jade along the way they laughed at Heather's boldness. It was hard for Jade to believe they were even talking about the same person.

From the time they got out of Erika's truck to the time they made it to the food court, Erika kept checking her surroundings like she was being followed by the FBI. Heather acting strange and the club vandalism had made her paranoid reacting to the situation completely out of character. If it were a few years ago she would have jumped at a chance to knock an enemy upside their head but being a mother and a business woman she decided to try and negotiate.

"I'm here now so tell me what it is you want," Erika said taking a seat. Heather wanted to meet in front of the food court so Erika was able to spot her quickly. She noticed that for Heather to be smoking crack she was rather healthy looking. Her makeup was flawless, her clothing complimented her body, and for once none of her acrylic nails were broken or missing.

"I see you couldn't leave your sidekick at home. What happened? I thought you were supposed to be a big movie star by now," Heather replied remaining standing as she cut her eyes at Jade.

"I know you ain't talking you bleach blond whore! Yeah, I know you used to jack those men off back in the day to get paid because you were too high to actually entertain a man," Jade said refusing the seat Erika pulled out for her. Erika and Jade were both witnesses to Heather's acts of desperation, lowering herself to jacking off her clients whenever they were bored with her and wanted to see another model. Funny thing is she barely received any extra money for her services.

"Jade calm down so we can see what she wants," Erika said having flash backs of beating the mess out of girl name Brandy who worked at the club. Negotiations were beginning to appear out of the question. Erika could almost hear the chant '*Whoop That Trick*' from the movie *Hustle and Flo* playing in the background.

"I know you don't want any of this Heather, so you better get to talking quick fast and in a hurry," Erika continued.

"Whatever, you owe me."

"What the hell have you been smoking to think I owe you anything?"

"Actually I haven't smoked in months and my mind is clear. You knew I shouldn't have gone to Nevada but you let me go anyway. You could have offered me a job on your sight," said Heather as she took a step closer to Erika.

Erika was trying her best to maintain her composure. Heather had really lost her mind fell off the deep end of the pool to think it was Erika's job to baby sit her. It wasn't like Erika told her to go anywhere, especially not all the way across the country to be a whore on a ranch who resorted to prostituting herself out to truck drivers. She could have gone to a strip club or another line of business for all Erika cared.

Laughing Erika said, "Now please fill me in on how things not working out for you in Nevada, being somehow my fault."

"You practically begged Jade to stay when she wanted to leave and I heard you tell my sister that you thought Nevada wasn't a good idea. You even offered both of them jobs but my sister wouldn't stay because of me."

"So because I didn't give you a freaking job I owe you like you were one of my employees anyway? Be serious, you have lost your mind and better find it quick."

"No, you owe me because some messed up stuff happened to me and my sister and now she is in a mental hospital. If you would have convinced her to stay she wouldn't have gotten raped and ended up there!" Heather replied matter-of-factly.

"You can not put that on me! It is sad what happened to your sister but I did nothing wrong. It was not my job to force her to stay. She is a grown woman just like Jade, who left as well," Erika answered defending herself against the outrageous accusations.

"Oh, Miss High and Mighty, you are going to pay one way or other whether you like it or not!" Heather said boldly pointing her finger at Erika's forehead just inches away from actually touching her.

Scooting her chair back, Erika rose up standing eye to eye with Heather sizing her up. She was sick and tired of her madness and drama. Erika was so close to her face that she could smell the ham sandwich on Heather's breath that she had eaten earlier.

"Come on," Jade said coming to Erika's aid, "let's go. She is crazy and is using a sad situation to get money. You don't owe her or her sister a dime."

Jade, holding onto Erika's hand brushed past Heather navigating through the crowd of shoppers. Jade was moving so fast Erika had to take extra long strides to keep up in her haste to put distance between them and Heather. The sale signs at Macy's, Victoria Secret's, and the Coach Store, which was something Jade never passed up, were nothing but a blur.

Slowing down once they had reached the ground level of the parking garage, Jade finally spoke, "I can't believe her. She is the one that needs to be locked up behind four padded walls, not her sister. I had to get you out of there before security had to pull you off of her."

"Was it that obvious?"

"Girl, Stevie Wonder could see the can of whoop ass you were getting ready to open. You didn't say much but your body language was telling on you."

Once her adrenaline slowed down Erika started to feel the pain in her right palm of her hand from her nails digging in her skin. Her jaw was also throbbing from clinching her teeth together trying to refrain from cussing Heather out in the middle of the mall. If she felt like a migraine was coming on earlier in the day, it was small in comparison to the pounding in her head. It felt like an aneurysm ready to explode at any given moment. She had to get a grip on things quickly before frustration and anger consumed her.

"You know what, she can be on her own island of madness but I am getting on with my life. I am not going to even worry myself about her. I am going to focus on having my club ready to go in the next month."

"I hear you. I see Xavier made it over," Jade said making note of Xavier's SUV in the driveway. "I will leave you two love birds alone. It's time for a shift change and my man should be walking out in any minute."

Ryan must have had ESP Erika reasoned because her front door opened and he walked right out.

"Later," Jade said leaving her friend in the vehicle alone.

Erika swallowed some Excedrin and chased it with water before heading inside.

"Where have you been?" Xavier asked as he gave her a hug.

"Me? I could ask you the same. Weren't you supposed to be here hours ago?" she countered a little angrier than she intended.

"Point taken," he conceded. "You seem upset. What's wrong?"

"Don't ask. Look baby I know we had plans but I need to just stay in and be alone to gather my thoughts."

"Are you sure?"

"Yes."

"Well alright. I don't like it but I understand. I am here if you need me. I love you. See you later." He said, giving her a peck on the lips.

The smell of stale cigarettes lingered in the air, long after he departed.

Chapter 10

"You like what I'm doing to you baby," Jade asked pulling down the top of her scarlet red mesh chemise. The mesh material was made to allow her breasts to be seen without pulling it down, but letting her DD's show without the material blocking them was to add extra delight.

Yes, Big_Bob2u typed.

Suck on them for me, he added.

Aiming to please Jade put the nipple of her left breast in her mouth suckling it then she released it letting her tongue flicker across the tip making sure to give a close up to the camera. Using both hands she caressed her breasts moving them closer to her mouth licking and playing with them moving them up and down like a girl jumping Double-Dutch.

Straddling the black leather chair like it was her lover she moved her body up and down riding it like a pro. Leaning back over the chair she maintained contact with her client moaning in delight. Knowing she had Big Bob's full attention she swung her body around facing forward to finish him off. Arching her back as she spread her legs open she removed her diamond studded thongs slow and seductive. Once they were off she used them as her prop sliding them across her flower making her nectar flow. With her juices flowing she dropped the thongs and proceeded to use her hands to pull her lips apart showing her inner pink walls.

"I want you to cum with me," she whispered.

I'm almost ready for you baby, he responded.

Leaving her inhibitions behind she rubbed her clit with a fierce passion letting the waves of ecstasy take over her body, making it quiver until she released on the chair.

"Mmmm," she moaned softly.

Knowing her show was about to end she rubbed her fingers in the juice she released on the chair. She then moved her hand closer to the camera giving her client a taste.

You taste delicious, he answered.

"Can't wait to have you again."

Session ended.

Jade was all smiles when she checked the stats on her show. Bob had stayed online with her for 35 minutes, and several men voyeured in sneaking peaks. That was one feature she loved about the site. When she entertained people in Free Chat and someone took her to a Private Show others always followed. At the club the men would have had to wait there turn and she would risk them going with someone else.

Jade called Erika after she freshened up from her show and when she opened up an envelop she received in the mail earlier. She opened it to be surprised by a hefty check.

"Girrrl, I love this job!" Jade exclaimed on the phone. "There is no way I would ever go back to letting men grope my body. This is easy money. I can't believe we used to actually do this in a club no matter how elite it was."

"I can tell. I watched your last three shows. You were really giving them something to make their mouth water."

"Yeah, but unlike the club I don't have to see them staring back at me as they jack off or risk them trying to rub their penis on my leg."

"Don't remind me," Erika said. "By the way you know I don't take any extra fees out your check. I only remove the amount for the shows. Now tell me the truth, Miss Nasty, were you putting on that last show for Ryan because you knew it was time for his shift, weren't you?"

"Naw, yeah…well maybe a little," she admitted.

"Girl please, don't be ashamed. Make that man want you even more," Erika joked.

"I learned it from you. But on a serious note, how is everything coming along with *Club Secrets*? You have been tight lipped about your plans for the past few weeks."

"Sorry girl, that wasn't my intention. With all the drama going on I have been playing catch up in order to have it ready in time. As a matter of fact you are interrupting me and Xavier's time right now. I will call you tomorrow, smooches."

Erika focused her attention on the sexy man massaging her shoulders. The stress from the club had her tense and Xavier saw it in her eyes the moment she opened the door for him. He had guided her to the couch, made her lie down and began rubbing the stress away.

Over the past few weeks Erika had her contractors on a tight schedule increasing their fee to meet her demands. She finalized her plans with the interior decorator and Kenny had finished wiring the rest of the club with monitors, networking them to her main computer at home. Getting her list of guests together for her grand opening consumed the rest of her free time. The only thing bothering her now was a call she was waiting on from the bank. Her report displays a breakdown on how many shows were purchased for the past month but the amount deposited in her account was a few thousand short. The bank was doing an investigation saying they would call her back in a few days.

After her massage, Erika rested her head on Xavier's shoulder as he watched the Colts third game of the season. They had a stellar pre season and were off to a wonderful regular season again this year. Normally Erika would have been into to the game as much as he was but her mind was focused on other things.

"Illegal formation? Man what where you thinking?" Xavier shouted at the TV. "Baby what do you think about having Monday Night Football at your club?"

"I'm not sure. That is a pretty big commitment on top of all of my other commitments, don't you think?" she answered enjoying the beer commercial. She didn't care for beer but their commercials always made her smile. Her favorite ones to watch were the Super Bowl commercials.

"Naw, I'm quite sure my business woman can set it up so one of the Hot 96.3 MC's would be happy to host it for you."

"I know but that's another meeting and contracts. I don't want to even think of that right now."

"Don't worry, I will handle it all for you," he said turning back to the game now that the commercial break was over.

"That's why you're my man," she said kissing him blocking his view of the TV momentarily.

"Did you see that hit? That was an excellent tackle. I can't wait to see it on Sports Center. I know baby, I'm the best," he answered not really paying her any attention.

She watched as Xavier went through the emotions with the players in the game. After a few more plays she made up her mind to get a little action of her own. Patting Xavier on the leg she nodded upstairs and mouthed to him that she would be right back.

In the privacy of her room Erika changed into her newly purchased lace baby doll lingerie in deep teal from Victoria's Secret. The catalog she ordered it from said it was a daring mix of delicate and racy. To make it more on the racy side she ordered it in the derriere-skimming length so Xavier would not have to guess at what her intentions were.

Tousling her shoulder length hair to make it look wind blown like the women in the magazine, Erika was ready to turn her night into one of passion and pleasure. Putting on some clear stilettos and a dab of *Very Sexy* perfume she went back downstairs to join her man.

Standing on the edge of the kitchen tile that connected to the living room she said, "Yooohooo."

"Hold on baby they only have 4 minutes left in the game," he started saying before he looked over at her. "Screw the game. That's what TiVo is for. I am all yours baby."

She held her position until he came over swooping her up into his arms. As bad as she wanted to have him take her to the room with the stripper pole she didn't want to take the chance of Kenny watching the camera and it would look obvious if she terminated the feed. Instead, she had him take her to the couch were she could give him a personal lap dance.

Changing the TV to XM radio, Xavier watched his baby move her body with the beat of the music. He watched as Erika rolled her hips like a trained belly dancer. The waves of her stomach drove him wild with lust. Moving closer she put her leg up over his shoulder, resting it on the couch. In this position he noticed she had on crotch less panties. Erika continued her dance by grinding her hips slowly and practicing a move she learned from Zane's *Sex Chronicles*. She squeezed her pelvis to make her vaginal opening move in and out taunting Xavier. He leaned in closer trying to put his tongue on it. Erika stopped him by lowering her leg and playfully slapping his hand treating him like a customer.

Almost exploding when Erika slid his jeans down taking his manhood in her mouth, he strained to keep it at bay. She was better than anyone her ever had. Without missing a beat she flipped her body around so his face was back between her legs.

"You are so bad," he murmured against her fruit before tasting her.

"Umm, Sorry," Asia said backing out the kitchen. She was taking a break in between her shows and walked in on their love making. The only reason she said anything was because she had the urge to join them. She was back up the stairs in a flash before they had a chance to respond to her apology. Watching Xavier's tongue dart in and out of Erika's nectar made her juices start to flow. She immediately went back on line so she could get paid to please herself.

"Oh my goodness! I forgot she was here," Erika gasped embarrassed.

"Oh well you are in the adult industry. Not like she hasn't seen it before."

"You so nasty," she replied gathering herself. "Let's take this party upstairs."

Xavier gave her more than she bargained for in a good way. After round three she had to concede defeat in order to get him to finally go to sleep. He sexed her so good her insides were sore. He took it gentle the first round but on two and three he was like a wild beast turned on by her pheromones. He laid sleeping inside of her until the sun peeked over the horizon sending a small beam of light through her blinds causing him to turn over on his back.

***

"I got some good news, Baby Girl! A buddy of mine has a cousin who is an MC at the radio station. He called him up and he agreed to host Monday Night Football at your spot. I still have to go over the contract but it is a lock," Xavier said.

"Wow that was fast. I can't believe you did it. Now my club is guaranteed to blow up becoming the hottest club in the Mid West," Erika said.

Xavier could feel her smiling through the phone. He knew his good news would be a pick me up for Erika who had been stressed about the club being ready in time and an ex acquaintance from her dancing days causing drama.

"Shouldn't I be there for the negotiations?"

"Come on now. You said you wanted me to handle it, so let me work my magic. You have enough on your plate as it is," he said reasoning with her.

"Yeah, I guess you're right. I just pulled up in front of Kenny's house. You still coming by later?"

"You know I am. So, what does Kenny want?"

"Not really sure. He said he wanted to talk to me about a few things. Who knows, it's probably some technical stuff about the website or the club. He always tells me about this stuff face to face so he can show me exactly what he means," she lied.

"Cool. See you later then, Sexy."

Erika sat outside in her car a few minutes before working up the courage to get out and knock on the door. Kenny hadn't said more than two words to her after she accused him of being jealous. He wasn't the one who wanted to talk, it was her. When he didn't answer his cell earlier she just started driving in the direction of his house. Being a Scorpio she had to maintain peace around her or she couldn't sleep well at night. Sucking up her pride, she walked to the door.

Hesitating a moment before knocking, she took a deep breath before going ahead with her plan to ambush Kenny into talking to her.

"Can I help you?" A caramel complexioned woman with flawless makeup and a freshly styled short hair cut asked, looking Erika up and down. The hair cut reminded her of the actress Nia Long when she played in *The Best Man.*

"Hello, umm is Kenny home?" Erika said trying her best to peak around the woman to see inside the house.

"And you are?" the Nia Long reject said folding her arms across her chest.

"Erika, his business partner, just tell him to call me it's important," she replied noticing the woman was not budging from the doorway.

"Okay," the woman said abruptly shutting the door, closing it in Erika's face.

Embarrassed Erika walked back to her car. Kenny wasn't jealous like she thought, he already had someone. *No wonder he hadn't called he was too busy getting his freak on,* she thought to herself.

I just wonder...do you ever...think of me... her cell phone played a song by Neo as she headed back out his drive way. She was embarrassed and in a hurry to get back to her side of town.

"Are you a stalker now?" Kenny asked.

"Stalker? Why would you say that?"

"You did just come by my house unannounced, did you not?"

"Yes, but I was not stalking you. I need to talk to you and you have not returned my calls."

"You have not bothered to leave a message for me to return your calls to answer you either. So what do you want to talk about exactly?"

"Who was that woman?"

"Are you the jealous one now? And I hardly doubt that was what you wanted to talk to me about when you were on the way to my house, seeming you did not know she existed until you knocked on my door," he said mocking her with his British accent.

"Whatever Kenny, look I talked to the bank and the totals from the site are not matching the deposits sent to them. They say it may be an issue with the site or with the merchant account holder. I also just wanted to talk about why we are not talking like we normally do, but you know what never mind I have my answer," she snapped.

"You seem to be so sure. In that case I will call you when I have the computers in the club fully functioning and when I check the site. Goodbye."

"Wait!" It was too late, he already ended the call. Knowing full well Kenny was not going to answer the phone if she were to call him back, she headed towards the Circle Center Mall to cheer herself up with a new pair of leather Gucci boots she had her eye on.

Erika spent over three hours in the mall coming out with not only the Gucci boots but a new black Prada purse, an outfit from Be Be's, two pair of Apple Bottom Jeans, a Movado watch for Xavier, and four Rocca Wear outfits for Shawn with matching Timberland boots. She had easily just spent over $2500.

Chapter 11

Jade stood outside of Xavier's office building watching as Ryan walked up. He had just come from the gym and was still in his basketball shirt and shorts. His muscles flexed with eat step he made, turning Jade on; making it all the easier for her to do what she had come to do. She gave him a devilish grin as he got closer, then held open the door for him to pass by. He only got a few steps before she pulled him into a unisex bathroom, closing the door and locking it behind them.

Passionately she kissed him, silencing the question trying to escape his lips. Jade slid her hands down Ryan's basketball shorts; allowing his already hard manhood to break free.

"Baby what are you doing?" He asked.

Ignoring his question, she swallowed the head of his penis causing it to get so hard she thought it would burst. She had an agenda; to make him cum and a short time to do it in. Going down deeper and harder on his shaft she over came the urge to gag. She wanted to feel all of him deep in her throat. Slurping and gurgling sounds echoing around the tiny space were soon drowned out by his moans.

What she was doing to him was driving him over the edge. He grabbed her by the hair, pulling Jade into him as he thrust his hips pushing himself farther in her mouth. She continued, taking it all.

Time is running out, she thought to herself. Using her right hand she grabbed his shaft and began rubbing. Sucking; stroking; and slurping became the rhythm as she continued with her mission.

"What are you trying to do to me?"

"You know what I am trying to do," came her garbled reply.

"It's almost there, baby!" Ryan cried out.

She had known already from the way his butt cheeks were clenched. Going for the gold she grabbed his butt; pumping him against her face while he started stroking on his own member. Focusing on the head she licked and slurped, licked and slurped.

Finally…he released her prize. It had been a week since they had sex so what came out was way more than she anticipated, but she did not waiver. She kept licking it until it was all gone.

When he was done, she rinsed out her mouth, with him watching.

"Damn, you are one bad girl," he said. He couldn't believe she had actually went through with his fantasy. When he told her about it he had no clue she would actually do it.

"I know, but I gotta keep you coming back for more," she smirked.

"I am not going anywhere baby, but I can't be late for this meeting. I will see you and her," he said pointing between her legs, "tonight."

"Yes you will," she mouthed back at him as he got himself together before leaving her alone in the bathroom. She straightened out her blouse and hair, heading out herself, not caring who saw her leave.

The janitor waiting to clean the bathroom held back his smile as she walked past him. He overheard everything. *And to think I almost didn't come in today,* he thought.

Jade's cell phone rang as she made her way to her truck.

"Girl guess who had a woman at their house the other day?" Erika said almost before the line connected.

"Well I know it wasn't Xavier because you aren't locked up," Jade laughed. "Come on you know I hate when you do this, just tell me already."

"Kenny."

"Kenny? I thought he was gay."

"Gay? Girl just because he is from Europe does not mean he is gay. He just sounds uppity. You remember when we went to the Bahamas last year and he got a rise from dancing close to me?"

"I remember you getting a lecture from him," Jade joked, "but seriously, who was the woman? Better yet, what did she look like?"

"I have no idea, but she was pretty."

"You didn't ask him about her?"

"That's the thing. He wouldn't give up any information. Hold on my other line is ringing."

Clicking over to the other line Erika said, "Hey baby, what's going on?"

"I got the contract for the MC and I'm on my way. I'll talk to you when I get there. I'm downtown and you know how my phone goes in and out," Xavier said.

"Okay, love you bye," she said switching back to Jade.

"That was Xavier."

"You need me to call you back?"

Telling her no, they continued talking for the next twenty minutes about Kenny and his mystery woman. Jade decided to keep what she had just done to Ryan a secret for now. She instead continued to instigate, telling Erika she should have knocked the woman over to see if he was in the house. Erika had to admit she was a little jealous only because Kenny had not told her about his new friend, not because she wanted to be with him. By the end of the call they determined they were going to find out who the woman was one way or another.

"I will talk to you later. Xavier just pulled up," Erika said before opening up the door for him.

Xavier was on a business call so Erika sat quietly reviewing the contract he handed her. She read over the first two pages and it seemed pretty standard until she got to the last page. In very small print it read, *In the event of cancellation 60% of fee is still due even if there was a 24 hour notice. Less than 24 hours would result in the full amount due.* After seeing that, she didn't bother to read any further.

"What's wrong," Xavier asked feeling her eyes on him after he ended his call.

"Did you read this contract?"

"Of course I did. What is wrong," he said taking the contract from her hands looking over it again trying to find what he had missed.

"He will still get paid no matter what if I sign this."

"That is standard for MC's, that's the only way they will agree to do anything now days. They have been burned too many times. You know they get offers all the time and once they agree to host something it takes them off the market for that time frame so I completely understand why it's in there," he said easing her mind.

"Well sense you put it that way I understand. Give it back so I can sign."

"Oh, that's the other thing. You wanted me to handle it so the contract is between me and the MC. It's no big deal because I'm representing the club for you, right."

"I guess you're right. I did agree to you doing it," she said cutting her eyes at him. She may have agreed but it felt like he was over stepping his boundaries. Then again she had been extra busy with getting the club open and her site lately that she wouldn't have had time to do it any way.

"You sure you are okay with it. I mean I can set you up with him if you want me too," Xavier said not missing the dirty look she gave him.

"No need, I'm cool."

"In that case I love you too," he said rapping his arms around her waist.

"You love me too? What are you talking about?"

"Hold on. I have to take this call," Xavier said stepping into the other room for privacy. Taking the call he returned in a few minutes explaining that he needed to make a run and would be back in a few. Xavier grabbed his leather jacket and left her sitting there.

She was in love with Xavier but wasn't ready to tell him yet. She was going to kill Jade if for letting the cat out the bag. She had been bugging Erika for weeks to tell Xavier, but Erika held her ground being stubborn like usual. Jade poked fun at her saying, "You can dance butt naked for men you don't know, but can't tell the man you care about that you love him."

"Jade," Erika sighed in the phone. She called her when the reality of Xavier not coming back hit her.

"What's wrong, chica?" she replied, picking up on the sadness in her best friend's voice.

"Do you ever truly think women in our line of work can be taken seriously or a man can truly love us and want only us, not the fantasy they want to fulfill?"

"Oh my god! You told him didn't you?" Jade knew the answer but wanted it confirmed none the less. Erika was hard on the outside but was really very sensitive when it came to someone she cared for.

"Yes."

"And?"

"And what?" He got a phone call right after he said he loved and then said he had to go," Erika answered.

"That's it?"

"That's what I'm saying!"

"No, that's why you are acting so melodramatic. Cause he had to leave? Girl, quit tripping. He said he loves you too. It will be okay boo. If not you know how we do, you Batman and I'm Robin. We can roll and bust out his wind shield, or slash his tires," Jade said trying to make her smile. She was really getting a kick out of Erika freaking out because she was in love.

"Shut up, fool," she replied, giving Jade the reaction she was looking for.

"Love you girl. Talk to you later. My man is calling me!" Erika could see Jade smiling through the phone. She was glad her best friend found happiness in Ryan.

What Jade said did make sense in a way to Erika but she didn't have anyone to compare a relationship too. Her father claimed he loved her mother and left her with five kids to raise on her own. He thought bringing gifts every now and then was his way of showing love. Her older brother says he loves his wife but other women constantly claim their kids to be his. Even her own son's father said he loved her, and as soon as he signed his name on the birth certificate he ended the relationship saying he wasn't ready to be tied down. She knew what love meant but was scared to find out Xavier's definition.

Xavier made his mysterious run, returning to Erika's house a few hours later. "You told me you love me on the phone before you hung up. I was wondering when you were going to admit to it," he smiled interrupting, her thoughts sensing her apprehension.

Erika could not believe her slip up. She remembered she did say she loved him when she ended the call. What surprised her more was that fact that he could tell all along and he loved her too. Stopping her from beating herself up, Xavier pulled her into his chest with his dark muscular arms. Smiling back she leaned into his warm embrace turning her head to the side excepting his passionate kiss letting her negative thoughts slip away. It was so peaceful sitting with his arms around her, she almost forgot about Kenny and his mystery woman.

Xavier's phone ringing pulled Erika out of his spell. Watching how he had a way with people as he talked on the phone she concluded that she did truly love him and was willing to trust him with her heart. She loved the way he licked his soft lips when he paused before responding to the person on the other line. She thought the indentation his dimple made even though he wasn't smiling was sexy. She noticed how his muscles seemed to jump out of his chest when he crossed his arms, and how his jeans seemed to be hand picked for him. What was between his legs would make a grown woman cuss out her own mama if she tried to stop her from getting it. She couldn't wait until he put that darn phone down because looking at him was making her hot.

As if reading her mind he hung up the phone walking over to where she sat on the couch and gazed into her deep brown eyes getting lost in them before he kissed her gently tasting the apple martini she just drank. Wrapping her arms around his neck she returned the kiss. Xavier then moved his mouth to the nape of her neck causing her to shiver.

"I have to go handle a few things I will be back," he whispered.

"You what?" she said pulling away from him pouting.

"I love you and I have to go," he responding kissing her on the cheek leaving her sitting in the living room feeling hot and bothered.

Staying put on the couch, Erika waited until she heard the front door shut and his truck pull off. For some reason she thought he would come back in saying he was only kidding, but it didn't happen. Xavier left her sitting alone twice in one day.

Chapter 12

"I'll see you when you get here," Erika said pressing the end button on her Black Berry.

Xavier had been acting secretive about his plans for her birthday, dropping hints for the past week saying it would be a night she wouldn't forget and to prepare for a mind blowing experience; anything to keep her guessing and frustrated. She told him from the beginning she loved surprises but Erika was driving Xavier crazy trying to find out what the surprise was. The more he teased her only added to her curiosity and made that super snoop side of her come out.

She had gotten so nosey she resorted to searching his truck and condo for clues. Anything would do for Erika a receipt, flyer, catalog or something with a name on it. The only thing she ended up finding with a Virginia Slim cigarette with some woman's scarlet red lipstick on it. When she found it she stopped what she was doing and stormed in the house.

"What the hell is this?" She said marching towards him holding the cigarette in the air with two fingers.

"A cigarette," he said smiling.

"You know what the heck I mean, sucka! What is it doing in your truck? I found it under the passenger seat. You don't smoke and you sure as hell don't wear lipstick." By this time she was standing in the kitchen, less than a few inches away from him with her arms crossed; tapping her right foot on the floor waiting for an explanation.

"This," he said taking the cigarette from her hand and tossing it in the trash, "is from a client."

Erika watched him, making a mental note to pull the cigarette back out the trash for a DNA sample and send it to this company online. She figured if they can tell who the daddy is then finding out who the woman was, would be just as easy. All she would need was something to compare it to.

"Yeah right, what was she doing in your truck?"

"You really don't remember do you? I was at Starbucks with a client when her Jag was repo'd right in front of me and Tyson. Heck you even called me when it was happening. She was going through a nasty divorce and her soon to be ex-husband stopped paying the note without telling her. Come to find out he cut her out of the business as well. I had to give her a ride home. You know I can't stand people smoking in my ride so I made her put it out as soon as she lit it. I thought she stuck in her pocket, not pitched it under my seat. I better not have a hole in my carpet."

"Sorry, I do remember. You forgive me," she pouted.

"Only if you quit snooping around, trying to find out what I'm doing for your birthday. You won't find a thing."

Her Private Eye career ended before it had fully started that day. Thinking about the event made her laugh. That was almost their first argument. It brought back an old memory about a woman she knew who used to smoking the same brand of cigarettes. Foxy, a chic from her club days used to smoke Virginia Slims all the time pretending she was a classy lady. She got drunk one day and started talking about men, comparing them to cigarette brands. Newport's were thugs and would get you caught up in the baby mama drama. Marbols' were ones who worked with there hands and could blow your back out having sex. Generic brands were the ones with no job and probably bummed the smoke from someone else; so he would be the one to try to spend a night one day and act like he's been living there forever; trying to sneak his clothes in a closet little by little. And finally the Virginia Slims, if he wasn't gay, this would be the fine brotha that would make you cum in your pants at the sight of him. He would tell you all the right things, treat you like a queen, and have the good paying career not a job.

"This one," Foxy said blowing smoke out the side of her mouth, "you have to be careful with. With the money and power he could be worse than the others and could end up killing you in the end if you became addicted to him."

"Dang that's deep. A man could eventually destroy you like a cigarette and end up giving you cancer. I am impressed," Erika said leaning back on the couch while they were waiting for their next client. She was shocked that Foxy could even rationalize something like that. The most things Foxy ever spoke of were her declining looks and making money.

While Erika continued to prepare for her evening she wondered how Foxy was doing now days. Before Foxy lost her mind, had her cousins rob the club, which resulted in Pops being accidentally murdered, she really wasn't all that bad.

Folding up her red lace teddy she planned on wearing for "Dr. Feel Good", her pet name for Xavier cause when he put it on her it felt so good; she placed it in her overnight Louis Vuitton bag along with her hygiene products. Staying all night was the only information he allowed Erika to have.

She did a twirl in her full length mirror in her hallway making sure she looked sexy in her little black dress, diamond circle of life necklace, and matching earrings. Her mother always said every woman needs a sexy black dress in their wardrobe because with the right jewelry it would be appropriate for any occasion.

Looking at her watch for the hundredth time she had a laugh at her own nervousness. "It's just for Xavier for goodness sake, calm down," she whispered to herself.

Her doorbell ringing almost made her heart jump in her throat. It was twenty minutes before he was supposed to arrive. Erika opened the door receiving an unwanted surprise.

"Going somewhere, bitch?" Heather hissed stepping a little too close for Erika's comfort.

"I don't have time for your crap today. What are you doing here?"

Heather started to speak, changed her mind and instead slapped Erika across her right cheek causing it to sting, turning her caramel skin bright red. Caught off guard but used to defending herself, she swung back hitting Heather smack dead in her eye. Thankful she hadn't put on her heels yet; she stepped to the side dodging a wildly thrown return blow from Heather. Heather lunged closer and Erika grabbed her head, ramming it into the door, leaving a dent.

Hearing the ruckus, Tyson the security guard on duty for the evening, came running downstairs pulling the girls apart. If he hadn't been so involved with watching the models seducing their clients, he would have seen Heather walking up to the house on the outside camera.

Pissed that she had been assaulted on her birthday, she refused to let go of the grip she had on Heather's hair. She was determined to snatch out every strand of her fake blond hair.

"Calm down, Boss Lady, I have her," Tyson pleaded, holding Heather in a headlock as she flailed wildly trying to free herself.

It was his first experience with a girl fight and he tried in vain to suppress his amusement. In the midst of the brawl Erika's dress had eased up, showing her red lace thongs while Heathers fake breasts were hanging out of her torn shirt.

"Please, this bitch had the nerve to come to my house, on my birthday! She will look like a cancer patient by the time I am finished with her," Erika spat, pulling out another chunk of hair.

Heather yelped from the pain of her hair being ripped out and was still in a daze from having her head banged against the door. Defeated, she slumped to the ground crying.

"She's dead," she said in between sobs.

"Dead?" Erika said letting go of the next patch of hair she was getting ready to yank out.

"Who died?"

"My sister, they killed her. They claim it was an accidental overdose but how could she have gotten extra pills? Melanie would never try to kill herself either. She was so happy the last time I saw her."

"Dang, I am so sorry," Erika said before she started to feel the stinging in her cheek; a reminder of Heather assaulting her with the drive-by slapping. Melanie's death was a shock and Erika felt bad for Heather; but right now she needed to get her crazy ass off of her property before Erika started wailing on her again.

"I can't believe she is really gone," Heather repeated over and over as Tyson ushered her back outside. He did not want to take the chance of them getting into it again.

Tyson shut the front door and faced Erika.

"Um Boss," he said uncomfortably nodding at her dress.

"Crap!" she said taking off to her room. Embarrassed she pulled her dress down as she ran. Tyson seeing her skimpy underwear caused Erika's face to turn redder now than what the slap had caused.

"Mercy, if that woman wasn't my employer…mmmph, mmmph, mmmph," he said shaking his head; converting the site of Erika's firm butt to his memory banks.

By the time Xavier had arrived, Erika had performed a miracle. She had covered up her bruised cheek, which was now hidden under a light powder foundation. She had no clue how, but her hair was a mess even though Heather did not get close to it. She put her freshly done ringlets up with bobby pins making a sleekly styled Mohawk. Nothing like what they wore in the 80s but the new runway type. Other than her dress being pulled up over her waist it was fine, no rips or tares.

"See that's why I love you. You look stunning and smell even better," Xavier said smiling as he walked in her room. Tyson had seen Xavier coming to the door and let him in. "Black is quickly becoming my favorite color."

"Why thank you. You don't look so bad yourself," she replied walking over wrapping her arms around his neck giving him a passionate kiss."

"Keep it up and we won't get to where we are going."

"Well I guess that means we better be on our way then," Erika stated. Not wanting to miss out on her surprise, she grabbed her purse and keys.

When they arrived Erika was in heaven. The Fondue restaurant was made for lovers. It was very intimate, with its high walls so you could not see the other guests, to the candle lit lighting. The person who was the architect seemed to have romance in mind when he built the building in a hidden area. It was on a busy street subtly placed between two larger buildings so it didn't stand out.

A vase full of a dozen roses and a card, with a poem by Maya Angelo, greeted them when they were seated at their booth. Xavier admitted to dropping them off before he picked Erika up. The waiter brought out her favorite drink without her saying a word. She was truly impressed with Xavier. For the past few years men seemed to disappear around her birthday or they were too broke to do anything like this. She had been lucky if they took her to the movies. When she left them; she normally went out and treated herself along with her girls.

Erika was so stuffed from the lobster tails, shrimp, chicken breast, and teriyaki steak that she thought she would burst if she ate the desert of strawberries, chocolate, and cheesecake that had just been placed in front of her. Nonetheless it looked too delicious not to at least have a taste. She read somewhere that good chocolate was almost as good as sex, so if that was the case then the strawberry dipped in chocolate she just ate had to be close to a screaming orgasm.

She sat back in the booth, relaxed. She was truly enjoying herself; so much that the incident with Heather was becoming a fading memory. She scooted closer to Xavier, giving him a kiss of appreciation.

Noticing the look of lust in Erika's eyes, he decided it was time to go to their final destination. Paying the tab he held out his arm for Erika walking her back to his truck.

"You need to put this on," he said handing her a black scarf to place over her eyes.

"I know you aren't serious," she said looking at Xavier like he was crazy.

"Come on, it's part of the romance."

"Let me make a call first."

Calling Jade, Erika told her, "Look I just want you to know that I am with Xavier right now. He wants me to put on a blindfold and if I come up missing he did it."

"Shut up fool," Jade said hanging up on her. Jade knew full well what Xavier was up to; she helped him plan it. Her friend deserved some true romance in he life.

"I know that you did not just call your girl on me like I am a serial killer. If I didn't want you so bad right now, I would leave your sexy ass on this corner."

"Oh really now," she responded running her fingers up and down his thigh. "I promise I will do whatever you say for the rest of the evening."

"Now that's more like it. Now will you please put on the blindfold?"

Without uttering a word Erika picked up the scarf, tying it around her head. She remained quiet the rest of the ride even when the ride starting feeling like a roller coaster. In Xavier's haste he picked up the speed turning corners so fast, Erika gripped the seat.

Erika was in pure bliss when Xavier removed the scarf from her eyes. He had brought her to the Sybaris, a fantasy hotel suite. The room had a king size bed with pure white bedding, covered in rose petals. Directly over the bed were several mirrors so they could look up and seem themselves having sex if they liked. Across from the bed sat a beautiful fireplace with a flat screen TV on the wall above it. The TV was hooked up to a top of the line surround system that could be heard throughout the entire suite. Exactly like the commercial advertisements, there was a nice size pool with a water fountain on the other side of a glass wall. The room had everything Erika could have dreamed of, even a fully loaded huge Jacuzzi on the edge of the pool.

Erika did not say a word until she had explored every inch of the room. Turning to Xavier she kissed him passionately saying, "Thank you. I've always wanted to come here, but never had someone I wanted to be with."

"Don't thank me yet. Thank me after I run this water in the Jacuzzi and feed my woman some cheese, grapes, and wine. You are my princess and that is exactly how I want to treat you," he said in a voice so deep and full of love. She knew he meant every word and so much more.

The red wine was a little too bitter for Erika's taste, but she didn't want to ruin the mood and swallowed the half glass he had given her in one big gulp. Waving him off on refilling her glass, she pointed to the cheese and grape tray he had prepared. Once they had their fill, he picked her up carrying her to the other room with the swimming pool. Laying her gently on the edge of the pool, Xavier placed his body on top of her making sure she felt how hard he had become.

"We can always go swimming later," she whispered turned on by his hardness.

That was all the hinting Xavier needed. He had been dying to taste her from the time she sat in his truck filling it with the scent of her perfume. He began sucking her nipples making them hard as ice to match his growing member. Placing one hand between her legs he rubbed on her bud with his index finger while inserting his middle finger inside her wet hole.

"You are so wet baby. You ready for me to taste you?" Xavier asked.

“Yes,” came her husky reply.

Xavier dove into her juicy pinkness licking and slurping his meal. He slid his body into the pool and pulled her body to the edge making her legs sit across his shoulders as he palmed her ass. There was no where Erika could run in this position; not that she would have wanted to.

“Mmmmm…ohhhh….damn baby!” Erika screamed between gasps of air. Xavier knew exactly when to apply more pressure with his tongue and how to nibble on her clit sending waves of joy through her body.

“You like how I eat this pussy?”

“Hell yes, baby! Don’t stop!”

Xavier flipped Erika over so he could view her body in the doggie style position. Her bud was completely swollen from the stimulation his tongue was giving it. If Xavier had his way he would eat her for hours savoring the way it tastes while enjoying the moans Erika let out. He continued with his feast by putting his tongue inside of her pumping away until her legs became weak causing her to sit on his face.

“Baby! I can’t take it any more. I need you inside of me,” Erika pleaded.

“No, I can’t believe I forgot!” Xavier said pulling away from her body. “I forgot to stop by the store and get some condoms, baby.”

"Huh, excuse me? Stop playing."

"Not playing. I was so busy trying to make this night special, that I simply forgot. I can run to the store real quick," he sighed not wanting to end their love making.

"Boy please you're not going anywhere until you make me cum," Erika said with a devilish grin. Taking Xavier's hand she guided it back to her wetness rubbing his hand across it. "Now get back to licking and insert one finger at the same time."

Doing as he was told Xavier made Erika cum in less than a minute. She came so hard she was scared she was going to break his finger the way her body was quivering, shaking and squeezing as she relished in ecstasy. He stood awestruck looking at Erika. His erect penis rock hard, pointing towards her; calling out for her to put her soft lips around it. Not wanting to leave him hanging she took his member in her mouth and before long he exploded all over her chest.

"Now you can go get the condoms."

"See, now that…that right there is the reason I am crazy over you girl. That was wild," Xavier smiled shaking his head at the woman in front of him. He rushed to get dressed and raced out the door. He had every intention of pleasing her more before the night was over.

Chapter 13

"I looked over your resume and it says you are a Human Resources Manager?" Erika questioned the lady sitting at the table with her. Erika had reviewed several applications and had not been impressed over the last few weeks. That is until she ran across one in particular. This one she decided to give a closer look. The woman living in town was a plus, Erika would not have to cover any travel expenses.

"You know you didn't have to submit a resume. Just a little background history and why you were interested in becoming a *Fantasy Girl,* would have been just fine," Erika continued.

"I understand. Is it going to be a problem? I just, well I have no experience in this type of thing at all. As matter of fact this is so not like me at all. The truth is I just got a divorce from my husband and I want a fresh start. He would have never agreed to anything like this," she replied quietly. She sat up straight in the chair, poised like she had been trained in charm school. Her short hair cut was simple, but cute. It was perfect for the corporate world. She wore makeup, not too much, just a little to enhance her beauty, and the outfit she had on was something Erika would have passed up in Nostrums. But there was something in this woman's eyes that called out to Erika.

"Well have you ever talked dirty to a man?"

"You mean like phone sex?" she blushed.

"That's close to what it's like. I mean have you ever told a man what you wanted him to do to you, or what you want him to do to you?"

"A little," she said smiling.

"Come on now. You have never told someone you were with that you couldn't wait for them to stick their penis inside you?" Erika whispered to the woman mindful of the other patrons. She had decided to meet her potential new client at the Starbuck's close to downtown because it was on her way to check out *Club Secrets.* Now she was beginning to regret it. She had no clue she was going to have to break down exactly what the models did on her site. Most of the people trying to join her site knew exactly what they were doing.

"No. I wanted to but I always let my ex-husband take charge," she replied honestly.

"Well honey, at *Fantasy Girls* you will have plenty of opportunity. I tell you what. I will look seriously into giving you a chance. In the meantime you need to brush up on your skills. Read some books about turning your man on and how to seduce him. This book I read by B. Swangin Webster has some good examples. Heck, even try those articles in Cosmo. As a matter of fact go to a strip club and get a lap dance."

"A lap dance? I am not gay?"

"Girl please, you do not have to be gay or bisexual to get a lap dance. It will help you learn your own body. Believe me I had to come out my shell too when I first got in this line of business," Erika reassured her.

"If you say so." She replied. The woman really was not sure, but she wanted this job and was willing to try.

"I will call you in a few days, okay. I expect you to tell me what you learned."

Erika was going to hire her, but she wanted her to loosen up just a touch first. She knew there was a freaky side to the woman and she was the one to help her bring it out and enjoy life. Those eyes behind the glasses and boring suit she wore were ready to break free.

"Thank you so much," the woman said. She stood up straightening out her skirt and adjusting her glasses before heading out the door.

Looking at her watch, Erika realized she was cutting her time close. She needed to get to the club to let in her deliveries in less than ten minutes. She hopped on her bike and took the back allies to her club. She made it to the back door of her club just as the truck was pulling up.

"You can park right here if you want," she said to the driver. You would have thought she was moving in slow motion with the wind blowing as she took off her helmet; hair flowing behind her the way he was staring at her.

"Oh yeah, here is fine Ma'am. I am looking for the owner. Is he here?" He said fumbling over his words when Erika walked towards him.

"She is here. My name is Erika, and I am the owner."

"Oh, umm, sorry. Well I am Jason and I have a delivery for you," he recovered.

He came down from the truck and handed a list to inventory while he unloaded her supplies. He remained quiet while he brought the items inside the club and put them by the storage closet. Some of her male employees showed up and started stocking the bar and putting the alcohol away.

“Thanks for coming Tre and Jay,” she said to her employees once they were finished. They were twins. She knew them from the gym where she was a member. When she saw them she knew they would be a must have at her club. She almost screamed out loud at her good luck when she found out that the both of them had a bartender’s license. When she offered them a job they were glad to oblige. They could not resist her batting her eyes and feeding their male egos.

“No problem,” Tre said.

“Do you need anything else?” Jay asked.

“No. That is it. Here you go,” Erika responded. She gave both of them a $100 bill before they left.

Erika finished doing a once over on her club. The alcohol had arrived on schedule, the bar tables and stools were all in place, the black leather seats had been installed along the walls closest to the dance floor and her two red round couches were in place on the other side. She couldn’t wait for tomorrow. If she was not so excited she would have allowed the disappointment of Kenny not answering his phone and Xavier pulling a no show to upset her. Erika gave the club a final once over before turning off the lights and heading home.

***

On the other side of town Kenny sat in a lounge chair positioned directly in front the stage. If Erika called him one more time he thought he would snap. He backed off on their friendship without giving her any explanation and if he talked to her today he still would not be able to give her the answers he knew she deserved.

He did not really understand why he hired a Private Investigator, he just did. And earlier today he got his answers. When he met with the Private Investigator it was hard to believe he had really gone through with his decision. It was so simple. He met with the PI, told her what he needed, and two days later he stood in front of her handing her the money. Kenny slid the PI the cashier's check for $1000 once he had what he needed. He couldn’t put his finger on it, but it was just something about Xavier that was nagging
at him. Xavier just happened to be there at the right moment Erika wanted to expand
her business and is way more than willing to help out, all the while
maintaining his own company. He looked at the contents of the envelope
before tucking it away for safe keeping.

Kenny took another sip off his ginger ale before focusing on the booty shaking in front of him. He was done being laid back and proper all the time. He couldn't take it any more; he had been watching the dark skinned beauty sashay around the club for the past hour. She was one of the sexist women he had seen since he started venturing out to Gentle Men's Clubs. He had been to a few but he liked the *Brass Flamingo* over the others. The girls seemed to be more friendly and willing to please. After seeing Asia's show earlier in the afternoon, he needed to feel a real woman against his skin.

Kenny was tired of using Astro Glide and the woman he was just dated turned out to be nothing more than a gold digger. He had caught her trying to pull up his bank account when he startled her by coming out the shower sooner than expected. He quickly got dressed and escorted her to his front door.

He focused on the dark beauty getting ready for the last song of her set to end. He wasn't looking to take anyone home tonight. He was not that type of man. Chocolate booty in his face was all he needed.

"How about a private dance?" he quickly asked Chanel as she stepped off the stage. He heard the MC say her name when he announced her coming to the stage.

"Sure baby. What's your name?" She said being polite. She could really care less but would at least get his name before taking all his money. She loved his type, very conservative and very big spenders.

"DJ," he replied adapting to the name he used at a few other clubs.

"DJ? You sure don't look like a DJ, but whatever you say baby," she said leading the way.

Watching her voluptuous yet firm booty cheeks bounce with each step she made had DJ's undivided attention. He barely noticed they made it to the back of the VIP area, which was located in the rear of the club.

Sliding off her stilettos so she would not accidentally kick him in the face; she placed them in a little cubby hole and began rubbing her breasts in his face. DJ fought the urge to suck on them and Chanel pulled back just before his resistance had worn off. Changing position, she slid in his lap and began a slow grind. When he looked down he could see her thongs shift side to side giving him a peek of her clean shave.

"Thank you," he murmured into her neck. He was turned on even more by the thought of diving head first between her thighs.

Feeling his manhood rise up, she thrust her hips back into him a few more times; then hopped up. Turning her thick, in all the right places, body around she then put her ass close enough to his face for him to bite into it. She placed one leg up on the chair while bending over making her ass clap and smacking it.

"I am so wet baby," she said over her shoulder.

"And I am so…" a smell assaulted DJ's senses so bad causing him to gag. He pushed her off his lap and ran out the VIP area, past the stage, and right out the front door. He could not believe the woman of his dreams for the evening had just let out a silent, but deadly fart in his face.

It was just as well because the woman he truly desired was with another man and probably would not give him the time of day if she were not.

Bzzzz, bzzzz his cell vibrated. It was Erika calling him again.

"Hello," he finally answered masking his annoyance.

"Finally, where have you been?" came the irritated response.

"I have been busy, Erika."

"So busy that you forgot to meet me at the club? It does open tomorrow."

"Tomorrow? I am so sorry I forgot. Is it too late? What do you need me to do?" Kenny was busy with the Private Investigator and got side tracked with the information he was given. He was genuinely sorry he let his friend down.

"It's too late. Everything has been taken care of. I really wish you were there, but it's all set up. It looks wonderful. You should see it. I am on my way home now, but please go take a look," she replied not hiding her disappointment.

"I will and once again I am really, really sorry. I regret letting you down."

"It's cool. I still love you. I have to go. I gotta get some sleep before my big day. I am exhausted."

Chapter 14

Erika could not believe her eyes when she pulled up in front of her club. Two news vans were parked in front of *Club Secrets* while another was across the street. About twenty women were marching with picket signs that read *No Prostitutes Allowed, Home Wreckers,* and it looked as if a few had a sign for banning (the circle with the diagonal line through it) smoking or something like it. As Erika looked closer she realized it didn't say smoking but had a black silhouette of a naked woman being banned.

The moment Erika stepped out of her car she was swarmed by news reporters and camera men.

"Miss Johnston is it true that *Club Secrets* is just a cover for your call girls?" a reporter asked shoving his News Channel 13 microphone in her face.

"No, it is a cocktail bar with a Gentleman's Club in mind," she replied overwhelmed. She wished the pavement would just swallow her up.

"Then why the private rooms with the love seats?" another reporter from Channel 6 demanded.

"Like I said, just like any other cocktail bar with something special for the men. It's designed to keep the more intimate encounters private. Someone wanting to spend time with a beautiful woman or get a private dance is just that…private. Where are you getting this information any way?"

Ignoring her question the reporters went on. "Miss Johnston are you trying to be the new Madam?"

"Isn't it true that you used to work at a club yourself?"

"Isn't it a fact that anything goes was the motto in another place you worked?"

Erika pushed past the over zealous reporters trying to go inside her club. They continued shouting questions at her back.

"Miss Johnston, allow me to introduce myself. I am the prosecuting attorney for Marion County," he said sticking out his hand and smiling for the camera's as if he was posing for the cover of *GQ Magazine*. "The city of Indianapolis will not allow something like this to exist. You will not tarnish our city's good name or embarrass our Colts."

"Your Colts? The players embarrass the team more than anything I could ever do. They stay in the news!" Erika said regaining her confidence with the Prosecuting Attorney. She had a grudge with them since the day they allowed her son's father to walk out of jail after serving 60 days and still not paying a dime of child support. Now he does not even bother showing up to court because he knows he will get locked up. They have issued a bench warrant but have yet to follow up with it.

"Nonetheless Miss Johnston or should I say Ecstasy, that is your stage name isn't it? The city has decided to lock your doors until a formal hearing can be done, which because of the back up in the court system won't be until at least 6 months from now," he replied in a voice of triumph stepping from in front of the door so Erika could see the chains on it.

"You Bastards! I have done nothing wrong! If I were a man you wouldn't even be thinking twice about this!" Erika screamed. She was livid, her body was shaking, she was breathing hard, and she felt her body going weak. If one more reporter shoved a microphone or tape recorder in her face she was going to punch their lights out.

A muscular arm reached out pulling her away from the crowd protecting her from the flash of the cameras with their body.

"Baby girl, you okay?" Xavier asked as he opened the door to the passenger side of his Tahoe.

Erika continued to get inside the truck in silence. She was in shock with a million thoughts running through her head. *How could this happen? How did they know particular details on the inside of her cocktail bar? How did they know she used to work at a gentlemen's club? How in the heck did they know what time I was going to show up?*

"It's going to be okay," Xavier said rubbing her leg as he drove.

Erika vaguely remembered the ride back to her house when Xavier startled her by opening her door. Gently lifting her from his truck he carried her into the house taking Erika to her bedroom. Placing her with her back facing the bed her removed her shoes one at a time then started rubbing her feet.

"I just don't understand how someone came up with the idea that I was going to have prostitutes at my club. My girls are purely entertainment not for sexual gratification, hell they aren't even getting completely nude. Nothing more than some beautiful women making some lonely man's day," Erika reasoned trying to figure out were she went wrong.

"Have you done something to anyone to make them want to get revenge?"

"Revenge, I haven't done anything to anyone. Heather keeps trying to get money from me saying I owe her. Oh my god, do you think it's her? That heifer don't know who she's messing with if she think I owe her something because I didn't hire her for my website. She couldn't be trusted to show up at *Passionate Playmates* half the time so why in the heck would I trust her?"

"Naw from what you tell me of her I don't think she's smart enough to go to the District Attorney. Definitely not if she's still on drugs," Xavier responded trying to have her focus on someone else.

"There is no one else," she said yawning.

"Don't worry about it then. This too shall pass. You're a smart girl you should have enough money saved up to start over, if it had to come to that. Now calm down and get some sleep before you give yourself an ulcer. I'm going to stay right here with you and keep you safe."

That was just like Xavier, always coming to her rescue a modern day Prince Charming. Erika could not imagine how she would have made it through the day without him by her side.

Erika tossed and turned all night long with images of being hauled off to jail. Once she got to jail they stripped searched her before spraying her down with a substance that smelled like bug spray. No matter how hard she screamed she was innocent no one came to her rescue. They locked her up tossing; away the key.

If she didn't have to get up and wire some money to her mother then she would have stayed sleep for another week no matter how many nightmares she had.

"What do you mean my account is frozen?" Erika questioned the ghetto-fabulous teller. This is why she hated going to the bank on 38th Street; but it was the closest Chase Bank to her house. Who the heck allows a bank teller to have her hair snow white on top and black on the bottom; resembling a skunk. To make it worse the teller had a gold tooth and long curved fingernails with wild designs on them matching her outfit.

"It says here, on the computer, that your account is frozen do to an investigation," Ms. Hood Rich responded as if the computer held the answers to all the worlds' mysteries.

Knowing better than to try and pry any more information from the teller, Erika took a seat in line to see the manager. Several equally ticked off customers were waiting ahead of her.

"Next," a skinny lady in a pink tweed business suit with her hair swept into a school teacher bun and black glasses sitting on the brim of her nose said. The lady looked as if she belonged in a corporate office downtown demanding someone to get her a latté rather than a manager of the small branch bank.

Following her into a back office Erika looked around at the plants and neatly placed pictures of the lady and her picture perfect family. The pictures were so perfect they resembled the ones that come in the frame when you purchase them from the store.

"So, Erika, may I call you Erika," she asked.

"Yes, that's fine. I want to know exactly why my account is frozen."

"It could be one to many bad checks or something to that matter," she said pecking on her keyboard.

"Oh, I really doubt that seeming that I have never bounced a check and I have over $350,000 in that account."

"I see," she answered looking at Erika over the rim of her glasses. "And how did you come into that much money? It shows here your funds are under investigation. The only other time I saw that; is when funds were achieved by illegal means. What is it you said you did again?"

Erika would have slapped the smirk off the stuck up lady's face if she wasn't holding her funds hostage.

"I didn't say, but if you must know I own an internet business and I just bought a building downtown. All of my money is by legal means, thank you. Now can you release my funds because I can show receipts, legers, and reports of my business dealings."

"Oh my, that's not for me to decide. You have to go to court for that. I hope you have a lawyer. Have a nice day," she said dismissing Erika as if she was an annoyance.

"Bitch," Erika mumbled under her breath, "you bet your $200 suit I have a lawyer."

Calling Keisha using speed dial, she had her sister put her boss on the phone. He said all of her business was in order and he could get her funds released but it would take some time because it was the DA's office who initiated the investigation. He advised her to get a lawyer and offered the services of his company. Erika already had one in mind, Angela, a mid thirties lawyer who was known in the office for never loosing a case and was a beast in the courtroom. She had even left a few judges speechless from her skills and knowledge.

In the meantime Erika pulled one over on the DA and had two other banking accounts opened as well as a money market account, once she was aware of missing money from her account a few weeks earlier. One account was in her mother's name and she was a signer and the other in her son's name. Her other accounts had over six figures in them apiece. She wasn't hurting for money, she was simply irritated.

"Xavier, my account has been frozen," Erika said soon as he picked up his cell.

"Frozen, did they say why? Do you need some money?" he asked a little too calm for Erika's liking.

"No, Keisha has me taken care of, and Jade owes me too," she replied lying. She didn't know why but for some reason she never told Xavier about her other accounts. Come to think of it the only person she told was Jade.

"Are you sure? I can meet you if you want me too."

"No I'm pissed off but okay otherwise. I have a few things I need to take care of so I will call you later," she said cutting the conversation short.

"What things? I'm free to go with you."

"I've been taking care of myself for a long time now. I will be okay baby. Talk to you later."

Erika didn't have anything other than wiring her mother some money to take care of. She just wanted a chance to gather her thoughts and sort things over. She moved like a zombie through the customer service line at Wal-Mart so she could send the money through Western Union. A vibration in her purse brought her back to reality.

"Hello."

"Miss Johnston, Edmond speaking. I saw you on the news. Looks like you are having a bit of trouble. I wonder who could have turned you in," he laughed.

"What they are saying isn't true and I have no idea who would tell those lies on me."

"No matter, I still want your business. It seems like you won't get to use it so I will buy you out. Otherwise you can wait months to fight to get it opened if the courts allow it. This being election year I seriously doubt if you will win."

"Are you trying to bully me into taking your offer?"

"No I'm simply stating the facts. You have no further use of the building so why waste your money."

"Screw you, Edmond," she replied tired of his condescending attitude.

"No darling that's what is being done to you. Now call me when you wake up from your childhood fantasies. They will never let someone like you own property downtown no matter what you try to do."

"Someone like me? What the hell is that supposed to mean?" she said. If the people in the Wal-Mart line were bored earlier they were definitely getting some entertainment right now. Erika was acting exactly like the type of person she couldn't stand, someone loud talking on the phone like no one else was around. The 'someone like you' comment pushed her past her boiling point.

"Young, a woman, black, must I continue? Call me when you see the world for what it is little girl," he said before hanging up the phone.

Everyone in the line was staring at her when she closed her phone.

"What?" She said to the prying eyes. "You act like you never seen anyone having a bad day."

Erika crumbled up her receipt, shoving it in her purse before storming out the store. If a bus came and ran her over she wouldn't have been surprised. Someone definitely had it out for her and she was going to find out who.

"Shayla, please take a look into my club and tell me who the heck is making inquiries into taking it over. Better yet, if you can tell me who the heck owns most of the downtown property. This jerk named Edmond is trying to bully me into selling him my spot," Erika spoke into her cell not giving her friend a chance to speak.

"Hello to you too. I saw the news and it looked like political B.S. to me, nothing more than a bunch of hype before elections. Who is Edmond?"

"Some bastard that I declined to let in on my business. I knew he was going to be trouble if I dealt with him. It's more than some B.S. They froze my account, but you know me I always have plan B. I started making withdrawals and changed where the website earnings were deposited a few weeks back when I noticed my numbers weren't matching up, but that is another story."

"Well I will see what I can find out for you. Give me a day or two."

"Thanks girl and sorry for sounding like a crazy person. I have just been going through some things," Erika said feeling bad for not even asking how her girl was doing.

"I'm your girl. If you can't complain to me then who can you? Now let me get to making some phone calls. By the way you may want to take a look at the newspaper," Shayla said.

Not quite sure if she really wanted to see the paper she hesitated before opening it. The front article was bad enough without going any further. It had the pictures of some ignorant people who held a Black woman hostage for over a week torturing her and doing unspeakable acts to her. Erika had seen a picture of the woman a few days earlier on the internet. The victim had patches of hair missing and she appeared mortified.

Turning the page Erika felt her knees go weak. In big bold letters the title read ***Seduction.com*** with an article that started off with, *the city of Indianapolis is not happy with* *idea of an ex-adult entertainer, who now owns an adult website, owning a club in the downtown area that could possibly be used for prostitution.* To make matters worse there was a picture of her being denied entrance to her club by the District Attorney. The only thing in her favor was she looked like a million bucks and she had on her oversized Chanel Sunglasses so no one could really see her face.

"Did you see the paper?" Erika asked Jade. Erika had called her right after reading the article.

"Girl, skip the paper you are on *YouTube*! People are making comments about how sexy you look and how they would do you if they had the chance. One comment even said how you should have decked the reporter that called you a whore. This whole thing has made you famous!" Jade exclaimed like Erika had just one the lottery and not been banned from a club that she owned.

"You are insane, you know that right. I am famous for all the wrong things."

"Please, you are nobody unless you are talked about. At least that's what that Hilton chic always says. Well forget what they say I am your friend no matter what happens."

"Gee, thanks," Erika said sarcastically. "I'm just happy my mom hasn't found out yet. Speaking of, she's calling me right now I will call you back."

"Hey Mommy!" Erika said answering her incoming call. She tried her best to put a little happiness in her voice.

"I got the money. Thank you. Now when were you going to tell me about these folks calling my little girl a whore?"

"Now where did you hear that Ma?"

"Just because I'm not into all the up today technology does not mean I don't watch the news. My baby lives in another city so I make sure I pay special attention to what they say is going on there. You may have had on those big glasses but I know my baby anywhere. I saw those signs they had in front of your club too," Momma Johnston said matter-of-factly.

"It's not as bad as it seems," Erika lied.

"You were a terrible liar when you were younger and the years haven't changed a thing. Saying you are trying to run a whore house is a very big deal."

"I know, but I have it handled. I hired a lawyer from the firm Keisha works at. She's a female with a name for herself in the business. Other lawyers call her a piranha in the courtroom."

"Do you need me to call her and tell her about the person my baby is?"

Erika actually let out a laugh. Her mother, bless her heart, always thought she could fix her problems like she was still in high school. She was always ready to call and talk some sense into someone to protect her child.

"Thanks Ma, but I can handle it. I am your child, remember? I can speak for myself now."

"But you will always be my baby. Well it seems like you have everything taken care of. I love you. Call me if you need me."

"I love you to, Ma," Erika said blowing her mother a kiss through the phone before hanging up.

Chapter 15

It appeared Jade had been right all along about *YouTube* was making Erika famous after all. Her site had tripled its viewers in the following weeks after her television fiasco. The men came to the site looking for her but found her girls just as pleasing. Technically the men did get to see her; she was the model on the flash page asking if the viewer was 18 or older to enter. The picture was of her in a black and pink Gucci Suit with a hat to match. The hat was tilted down covering her right eye while her hair was in long curls cascading down her back. To put a twist on the look her top was unbuttoned showing a hot pink Victoria Secret's lace bra. She came up with the idea from Beyonce's *Upgrade You* video, when she was pretending to be Jay-Z. She loved the style because it showed her sexy and powerful at the same time.

“Hey, Boss Lady. I have another application for you to look over,” Ryan said.

“Really,” Erika smiled looking up from the court documents she was going over. Angela had them set to her via courier. The DA was wrong in his assumption about having to wait six months to go to court. It seemed as if a well known judge was a regular to her old club *Passionate Playmates* and was an elite member of *Fantasy Girls* who was more than willing to pull a few strings. Her lawyer was informed of a court date in less than four weeks.

“Yeah, I think she is from Brazil or something. She is beautiful and her name is Ananda.” The smile on Erika’s face let Ryan know he had done good. He hated to see Erika down with all the stress she was going through with the club. He was even looking forward to working with her there as well. Erika paid well and caring about her employees was a big plus. He also had learned his lesson, responding quickly to the Plain Jane’s by deleting their applications. He brought an average looking girl to Erika once and was asked would he spend money on her. When he hesitated Erika tossed the application in the trash without a glance. She informed him that if a woman did not catch Ryan’s eye, then what was the chance of the girl pulling in big money. After all, her site was named *Fantasy*

Girls, not the girl next door. Erika did not want to be like other sites. She wanted quality, not quantity.

"My, she is gorgeous," Erika said looking at the picture of the girl. She admired the confidence of the girl for sending professional pictures instead of the ones she usually received from a cell phone or web shot. Ananda's background scenery was on a beach causing her flawless bronze skin to glisten in the sun. Erika wasn't quite sure but her eyes seemed green, almost like an emerald.

"Well I see she has a home computer and does not need a studio. Email her back to see if she can be ready in an hour. I want to see what she is really working with. I will give Kenny a heads up as well." Erika was already typing a text message to Kenny before Ryan walked out the room.

Hey I have an exotic Brazilian wanting to join the team.

Nice, tell me when and I will be online. Kenny responded.

20 minutes, she sent back.

She secretly wished that Kenny was with his new love and had to interrupt their time with him working. Erika wasn't the least bit jealous but after the nameless woman (Kenny still had yet to introduce them) slammed the door in her face, Erika enjoyed the thought of getting under her skin. But with the way Erika's luck was going lately the woman probably would enjoy watching the show with Kenny.

She better not, Erika thought to herself. *That is unless she is gonna pay for it.*

Erika ate a quick snack before heading up to her office in hopes of seeing a good show. Some Brazilian flavor would be sure to peak the interest a few of her high rolling clients.

"Well I see she's all ready to go," Erika remarked noticing that Kenny was already online explaining the process to Ananda.

After a few moments the show was ready to begin. Ananda sat facing the camera showing a beautiful smile in a black top that tied in the front to cover her breasts and black booty shorts to match. Her breasts were so full they were barely staying in her top. She grabbed her breasts and flipped her hair, then went back to sitting there smiling to the camera. Erika heard someone speaking who wasn't in the view of the camera, at first she thought the girl had company, and then she realized it was her television.

"Turn the TV off please," Erika told her, "and put on some music." To be sure the girl understood her she clicked the translate from English to Spanish button and sent the message again. The translator was a big help because a lot of girls were complaining that they could not understand their customer's who were in other countries. Now a simple click helped the communication gap. The translation was a bit off its wording at times but, it was still able to get the message across.

Before long *Girls, girl, girls, girls* by Jay-Z filled the room, replacing the Spanish Soap opera playing in the background. The song was old but it was a fitting choice for the lovely lady on the other side of the web cam. It took some time but Ananda finally started moving to the music and actually became enjoyable to watch. She was truly an amateur resembling Jamie Lee Curtis dancing in *True Lies,* but at least she was moving and following Erika's guidance without question. Erika knew she had a winner when Ryan quietly excused himself to the restroom. Erika took notice of his bulge on his way out.

"Good job," Erika said. She was thankful that Ananda decided to put in some effort instead of just being a smiling sexy face. She already let a few girls go from one too many complaints from her customers. After watching some of the private shows, Erika sided with the clients and the girls had to go. For twenty minutes or more the girls just sat on camera doing absolutely nothing; not on one or two, but on all their shows for the day. The men were lucky if they got a flash of vagina. Erika was not in the business of ripping men off. Therefore, after firing the girls she posted a bulletin letting all the other models know that if they chose to behave the same they will get the same results. Once those girls realized that this was easy money and had to get other jobs or go back to whatever else they were doing, they would beg to actually entertain a man who could not put a hand on them. Of course they may find something better but Erika doubted it because none of her models pulled in lest than $6000 take home a month.

One other plus for Ananda was that Erika did not have to advise her to shave or trim up her goodies. Ananda had a trimmed trail of hair leading down to her shaved vagina. Erika generally didn't like to get in the model's business like that but she had come across a few beauties that haven't trimmed a hair from the day it started growing. Hairs were so wild they were hanging out their thongs looking hot and funky. The funny thing is a small percent of men like it, but it was not enough to turn a profit when it came time to crunch the numbers.

Kenny emailed Ananda the payroll forms once Erika gave him the go ahead that Ananda would officially be a *Fantasy Girl.* Grateful for the break, Erika reluctantly went back to reviewing the court documents and her awaiting tension headache.

From the content of the papers the DA was trying to go after her no-holds barred. Their main evidence was her former job and her current business. On paper it looked bad but Erika had never been a prostitute nor would she ever be a pimp. She didn't even let her girls go on dates or take outside gifts from the clients. If she found out that one of the girls did then she was put on probation. She wasn't too worried about her online business but the club would be another issue, harder to prove nothing went on behind closed doors. With the club being closed she had no proof and she knew the judge who got the date pushed forward was not going to admit that he was a valued customer.

Miss Independent by Neo started playing on Erika's cell phone distracting her once again from her mounting head ache.

"Hey Kenny, what's up?"

"I thought you would have at least called me back by now. Did you forget something?" He asked patiently waiting for her reply.

"Let me think. Naw, not that I know of. Everything is straight with Ananda right?"

"Yes, but I was not referring to the business aspect."

Erika hated the guessing game and hated Kenny never loosing up even more. It was just the two of them on the phone yet he was still being so formal.

"You don't remember what today is," he continued. "It is my day of birth."

"Oh man. I am so sorry. Happy birthday! What can I do to make it up to you?" Erika asked feeling low for not remembering.

"Well, you are forgiven…under one condition. I want you to take me to a strip club."

"Are you serious? What about your new love?" Erika teased.

"We are no longer together and I will tell you about it once we are at the club. I will be by to get you in an hour. Bye." He said abruptly ending the call.

Erika could only look at her phone and smile. She was quickly realizing there was more to her friend than she thought. It was a good thing that Shawn was at his father's house for the weekend, otherwise she would have had to call Keisha and she would have wanted to come along instead of babysitting. She wasn't quite sure how Kenny would feel about extra company. It was amazing how D'wayne finally wanted to actually take his son with him for the weekend. He seemed to be concerned with her situation asking if her finances and business were going to be okay. She didn't answer figuring if he really cared he would pay his child support.

Changing out of her sweat outfit and into Coogi Couture jean pants and top, she was ready just as Kenny was ringing the doorbell.

"You look nice," she said giving Kenny the once over. He was wearing a Sean Jean sweater and slacks with a leather hat to match. He even found some nice shades to go with it. "I am impressed. You ready?"

"Yes," he said taking her arm leading her to his BMW.

"When you get this?"

"Just this morning. It is a present to myself. As they say, I had to upgrade," he replied grinning from ear to ear.

Erika sank into the leather seats admiring his new style as they rode in silence to the club. The new car smell as well as Kenny's cologne was soothing to her senses. The smooth jazz CD added to erasing the last bit of tension she felt slipping away.

Kenny paid their way into the club and Erika led them towards a nice table so they could see all three stages. The main stage had a runway leading to the pole and the other two were circular stages with poles in the middle. It was a busy evening already because all three stages had girls on them. She and Kenny filled the last seats in the place.

"Please call me DJ while we are here," Kenny leaned across the table telling her once the waitress walked away.

"DJ? Do I want to even know?"

"I always thought of my name as well, plain. I wanted to try something else for the evening. Besides I thought you would like it because that is name of that actor you adore,

Terrence Howard….my look at the rump on her," Kenny trailed off. His eyes were too busy focused on one of the strippers walking by. The girl had a small waist and hips but the ass on her was out of control. It was so big that it hypnotized everyone in the room in view of it.

"Now coming to the main stage is Sensation!" The DJ screamed into the microphone hyping up the already intoxicated crowd by putting on *Low* by Flo Rida.

She got them Apple Bottom jeans and the boots with the furs…the whole crowd was looking at her blared throughout the speakers giving Sensation a boost of energy. She grabbed the pole with one hand, swinging around it, flipping herself upside down then back upright almost as if she was a trained acrobat. Using her arms only she slowly glided down the pole moving her legs in slow motion like she was riding an invisible bike. When she was close to the bottom she let go smacking the ground landing in the splits. Sensation was nowhere near finished with the crowd. She started making her booty bounce in that position sliding across the stage to one of the customers sitting in the chairs around it. Doing a forward flip she rolled tossing her legs over the shoulders of the man, her privates inches away she did some pumping motions almost giving him a mouth full. Tucking a five in her thongs the man laid back with a look a love on his face while Sensation moved on to the next victim.

"Did you see that?" Erika said to an empty chair. Kenny aka DJ had snuck off, pulling up a front row seat at the stage. Erika spotted him at the stage moving his head to the rhythm of Sensation's bouncing ass. She was facing doggie style and her booty was putting in overtime. As it bounced to the music she slid her body to the end of the stage and into his lap face first with her crotch up in his face. Sensation booty pumped his face while rubbing her face in his lap. DJ was so in awe Erika wasn't sure if he knew he had just tucked a $50 bill in Sensation's booty crack.

When Sensation was done with her set DJ was the first in line to get a private dance, not the $20 lap dance, but the $100 dance in a side room. Erika smiled and waved him off continuing to enjoy the other dancers on the stage. The club had a variety of dancers ranging from several nationalities to different ages. There was one dancer who had seen her last days ten years ago but it didn't stop her from trying. She walked around the pole a few times making a few stiff twirls. A few men tossed some singles out of pity. Erika was grateful when her turn was over and she exited the stage.

"You wanna buy me a drink?" A cute biracial dancer said plopping down in Erika's lap.

"No, and are you old enough to drink?" Erika said patting to the chair next to her so she could get a better look at the girl.

"My name is Jasmine and I am 22," she responded smiling like a cheerleader performing in the state championship game.

"Nice to meet you. I'm Erika. How long have you worked here?"

"A few weeks. You are very sexy. You should work here," Jasmine beamed inching closer, closer than Erika preferred.

"No thank you. I am in the adult business. It's online. You should check it out." The girl was sexy enough to be on Erika's site and she was always looking for new talent.

"First," Jasmine said feeling on Erika's breast, "you need to check me out." With that being said she moved her face between Erika's legs and blew on her crotch instantly warming up Erika's body.

"Umm,wow!" Erika responded flustered digging in her purse for some money. She pulled out a $10 stuck in Jasmine's garter belt and sent her on her way. "Shit, now I know why Kenny was in the VIP area. That was a slick move."

Not to be caught off guard again Erika crossed her legs any time another dancer got close to her and sipped on her drink until Kenny returned 45 minutes later. She saw him floating through the crowd like a Spike Lee movie coming from the private area.

"I take it she was worth every dime?"

"Yes, and I am ready to leave whenever you are," he said still beaming.

Erika finished off her drink and they headed to the car. Kenny/DJ could not stop talking about this being a birthday to remember the whole ride home. When they reached her house Erika gave him a hug wishing him happy birthday once again before going inside. The subject of his girlfriend dumping him never made it back into their conversation.

Chapter 16

"Did you see your baby mama on TV? She looked pretty," Tina asked interrupting D'wayne watching *Sports Center* on ESPN.

"How could I miss her? That's all they have been talking about for weeks now. And why do you care about her any way?" He replied agitated she was causing him to miss the highlights.

"I mean Erika never did anything to me. She is always polite, and you have to admit she has it going on."

"So what? Are you her agent or something? You act like she is Kim Kardashian or somebody. You wanna go work for her now too? Go ahead put yourself out there for every man to see your fat roles and stretch marks," D'wayne snapped back. He pointed the remote control at her pushing the power button in hopes that Tina would get the hint and disappear.

"Why you have to be so mean?"

"Why you have to be so stupid? You will never be like her so quit dreaming. You plan on going to college now and getting a degree like her too? Please you barely finished high school."

He really didn't intend for that to come out, but it did. It wasn't her fault she got stuck at home watching her brothers and sister's while her mother disappeared for days at a time. He was just sick and tired of hearing about Erika doing well. He couldn't believe how she showed up dressed to her club, an expensive business suit and sun glasses. Did she think she was in Hollywood or something? She sure as heck wasn't going to a business meeting. No matter what she wore or what degree she had; in his eyes she was still nothing more than an overpaid stripper.

It was bad enough that when he checked his email someone forwarded him a *YouTube* link and it was of her trying to get into her building and all the reporters' surrounding her. Someone did a voice over and when everyone spoke it was like a bad porno. He was pissed that he had just been added to the other 150,000 hits. Now Tina had the nerve to say her name in his house. It was really Tina's house, but he contributed whenever he could; which wasn't very often.

"I am leaving. And you can kiss my fat ass goodbye!" She screamed; snatching up
her purse and storming out the house.

"Yeah and when you come back make sure you bring me some food."

"When I get back your ass better be gone," she hissed under her breath. Lately D'wayne had been acting strange every time Erika or his son was mentioned. She was on to his tricks about not wanting to spend time with Shawn months ago. She asked D'wayne about getting his son for the weekend, so he said he would call. Then, Tina pretended to give him some privacy, went upstairs picking up the other phone line. She overheard Erika telling him it was okay to pick Shawn up and asked what time was he going to be there. But when he got off the phone, he lied and said she had told him no.

When she confronted him about it he gave in. He went and picked up Shawn from Erika; spend two hours with him, before dumping him off at his grandmother's house. D'wayne claimed he had plans and Shawn was not about to get in the way. She hated how he wasn't a good father, but most of the time he was good to her. Besides she hadn't had a man in her bed in a while and he had been good company.

But he can hang that crap up cause I am not going to be disrespected. Heck there may even be some men that will pay to see my rolls, she thought to herself as she drove away. She was far from obese but a little work on the few extra pounds she picked up from having her daughter four years earlier couldn't hurt. And if D'wayne paid her any attention he would have noticed that she enrolled at Ivy Tech Community College weeks ago.

***

Since Erika was still restricted from getting into her club she turned all of her focus to her website. She made sure she had not overlooked anything her girls were doing on the site. Security did a good job, but it was not up to them to make certain decisions when it came to
the girls not following the rules, scheduling their days to work; if they were using Erika's house; and they could not hire anyone.

After her last suspension Diamond seemed to have gotten her act together. She was
chatting more with the clients and even giving small dances in Free Chat. Diamond may have lost some of her old fans to other girls, but she sure gained new ones. For the day alone; she had 23 previously recorded sessions downloads. Erika was thankful that Kenny went with her idea and

updated the site to allow people to be not only being able to look at a girls profiles, but purchase the shows they missed or wanted to see again. This way a model could still make money without being online.

After checking the models, she started scanning the site users to see who were some of its' consistent big spenders. When she narrowed it down to the top two; she would give the customers discounts, freebies, or whatever special thing she came up with that month. When she finished she looked to see who the monthly offenders were; the users who got kicked out of the girls' rooms. Two names showed up at the top, DevilDog and The_Generious1. They seemed to have gotten kicked out of almost every models room on the site. This was very odd because most of the men got their act together after the first or second ejection.

She clicked the file open to see what the reasons were for ejection and to her amazement they were almost all the same. The two users, who were more than likely the same person, wanted the girls to be very x-rated in the free chat rooms and encouraging them to switch over to another site.

Of course they would have to switch because they would get suspended or fired doing any of the crap those two clients asked for.

He asked some of the girls to put their toy inside of them, others to use their fingers if they didn't have a toy, if it were two girls in the room he would ask them to lick each other. Some of the things were normal comments that guys made, but it was the way they did it; as if it was an interview or something. Kind of like; show me what you have and I will hire you on my other sight; type of deal.

A light bulb when off in her head. She went back in the archives and found what she was looking for. MsWorkIt's user log the day she lost her mind and Erika had to fire her. Sure enough The_Generious1 was in the chat room with her.

What a dummy? She was willing to loose her job because someone gave her an empty promise to go to work on another site. And none of the sites pay the girls close to what I am paying. She knew this from her own personal research. Some of the sites
weren't even giving the girls half of what they brought in, more like 20-30%.

"Hey sis, you busy?" Keisha said poking her head in the office.

"Just finishing up. What's up?" Erika replied, looking over the top brim of her glasses. She had not bothered to put in her contacts. Her hair was wrapped around a pencil and stuck up in a bun. She looked like a naughty teacher. The ones all the boys fantasized about in junior and senior high.

"I went over your case myself even though I am not assigned as the paralegal and you have absolutely nothing to worry about. The Prosecutor's Office has way bigger fish than you to worry about. And on a lighter note you need to get dressed so we can go hang out. Me and Jade have something planned for you big sis." Keisha said smiling.

"Oh really?" Erika said logging off her laptop.

"You have 30 minutes," Keisha said moving out the way for her sister to get past her on her way to her bedroom.

After Erika got dressed she rode with Keisha over to Club 300. Erika normally didn't hang out there unless it was a special event because the place was small; nice, but very small. She noticed that the parking lot was packed with cars.

"What is going on up in here?" Erika inquired after seeing the crowd.

"I have no idea because we are back in the VIP room," Keisha laughed, grabbing her sister's hand and pulling her past the men starring them down.

"Hey, sexy Lil Mamas, where you in a rush to go?" someone asked as they brushed past. Erika would have stopped to chat but Keisha had a tight grip on her.

The VIP room was packed with nothing but women and a pole was set up in the middle of the room. Erika started to protest until the MC cued the music and three fine specimens came out a side door. One was 6ft 2in, brown skin, body like an African Prince, and dressed like a fireman. The other one she wasn't quite sure of his nationality, but she was quite sure he had some Asian in him; was dressed as an Indian. The feathers on his g-string barely hid anything. And the third was a one of the finest Caucasian men she had ever seen. He was dressed like a construction worker in cut off shorts, and hard had.

Just as Erika was wondering where Jade was hiding, she saw Jade dragging a chair towards the center of the room. Instead of coming over to where Erika was, Jade left the chair were she stood, smiled at Erika, then walked in the other direction. Out of the blue the men surrounded Erika, picked her up and walked her over to the chair.

"Oh no you don't," Erika said trying to escape. Erika was used to dancing for men but getting one from a man as sexy as these was hard for her to take.

"Where are you going baby? You are ours tonight." The fireman said pushing her back in the chair. The construction worker got behind her and began rubbing her shoulders, while the Indian started hypnotizing her with a slow grind in her face. He began working his abs and flexing every muscle in his chest and thighs.

“If she don’t want it, I’ll take it for her!” a female shouted from the sidelines.

“Oh she is going to take it,” Jade said coming up behind her. She pushed the construction worker aside and began tying Erika’s hands behind her back with a scarf. “You will take it and like it.”

Once Erika’s hands were secure, it was game time. The fireman put his crotch right in front of her and rubbed her face in it; his manhood rising in the process. The construction worker went underneath the fireman and put his face directly between Erika’s legs pretending to taste her. The women began going wild, screaming all calling for the men to let them join in.

The Indian gently slid her arms from over the chair, careful not to remove the scarf. He lifted her up in the air, putting her crotch in his face. He blew on her and made exaggerated slurping sounds before flipping her around and putting her on the ground in the doggie position. The construction worker adjusted her body so she was straddling him and the fireman took his position in front of her face. With the Indian still behind her he pumped at her from behind causing her to go face forward into the fireman crotch, while grinding down on the construction worker lying beneath her.

Erika thought she was going to die. She was so embarrassed, but the other women loved every minute of it. She looked as if she was being sexed by three men at the same time.

For what seemed like an eternity but was really like another five minutes; the men took their time working her over and playing to the crowd. When they were done they finally untied her hands leaving her standing in shock. Jade saved her by pulling her off the floor.

"You are so going to get it," Erika said playfully poking Jade in the ribs.

"Don't act like you didn't enjoy every minute of it."

"Yeah, I did but it was so embarrassing. Where is Keisha?"

"Child please, she and the rest of them women jumped on that eye candy two seconds after you stepped out the way. Look at them."

"I don't know half these folks. How did you pull this off?" Erika asked taking a good look around the room.

"You not the only business woman in the family, Keisha put this together. She made flyers announcing a pole party and male strippers. Admission was $20, which with all these woman it will not only cover the room, the MC, and strippers, but put some money in her pocket as well. All I did was help get the word out. She was tired of seeing her big sis mope around," Jade replied giving her a big hug. "Oh and if you didn't see her, Shayla is up in here too."

Erika spotted Shayla waving her money at the stripper dressed as the Indian. He was earning his money by turning Shayla around and grinding his pelvis up against her ass like he was giving it to her good. When he was finished she tucked the bill far down in his g-string; far enough down for her to get a good look and feel.

"Well I know exactly were she is and will be for the rest of the night. So when does the pole party start?"

"Um, well it already ended. We figured you had more than enough skills on the pole and didn't need to come outdo everyone. So we brought you out for the main entertainment," Jade said backing back to avoid another jab or pinch.

"I would be mad, but I don't think I could have stomached some of these big woman or these old crows trying to get up that pole," Erika replied laughing.

Jade turned her attention back to the men as Erika pulled out her phone to check for missed alerts. She had one text from Xavier that said when she was done enjoying herself to come back in the main area.

"Jade, Xavier is on the other side I will be back."

“No you won’t. I knew he was here. Enjoy your evening, as I will definitely finish enjoying mine,” Jade said with a devilish grin.

“Tell Shayla thanks for coming, even though I didn’t get to talk to her.”

“Sure, now go on. I have some ass to grab,” Jade responded shooing Erika away.

Erika walked in to the main portion of the club, spotting Xavier right away. He was sitting at the bar sipping on a drink.

Those men were fine, but they have nothing on this man in front of me.

“Hey baby, what are you doing here?” She said after giving him a peck on the lips.

“Waiting for you. I have to get some quality time. I can't let the girls have all the fun,” he replied, eyeing her outfit.

“So you knew about the male strippers?” She asked, not quite sure on how he would react.

“Yeah, and I also knew that you were coming home with me,” he said with confidence.

“Oh really? So are you ready now because this is really not my type of crowd."

The club had a majority of college kids and Erika preferred the professional crowd. That way she could party and network at the same time.

He answered her by gulping down the rest of his drink, closing out his tab, and escorting her back to his truck. When Keisha first informed Xavier about the party, he was cool with the whole male stripper thing but the longer he sat around the more his mind began to play tricks on him. He had visions of them rubbing all over his woman. If she had stayed in there any longer he was sure he would have went in after her. She didn't know it at the moment, but he was going to put it on her so good that it would erase all the memories of those men.

Erika gazed at Xavier while they sat at the light. He looked magnificent with the light from the moon reflecting on him. The embers between her legs were still warm from the fire the strippers had started. Leaning closer she gently grabbed his chin, pulling his face toward her. She nibbled on his bottom lip then gave him a deep longing kiss. Angry passengers started blaring on their horns. Reluctantly ending the kiss, Erika noticed the green light. Without taking her eyes off him, she leaned back in her seat.

That was all Xavier could withstand. He whipped the truck, making a left turn. He drove three more blocks and pulled up at a neighborhood park. He followed a path a little ways before parking. Getting out his truck he walked over to Erika's door and opened it. He put his mouth on hers; kissing her with shear passion. Inching his hand down her pants he found what he was looking for. He felt it. She was hot, wet, and ready for him. Erika kicked off her heels and lifted up her hips, making it easy for Xavier to unzip and slide off her outfit. He wanted her black and silver, one-piece suit off her the moment he saw her in it. The outfit had her succulent breasts ready to spill out the top, while it hugged her hips and curves, taunting him with every move she made. Once he freed her body, he tossed Erika's clothes in the back seat. Her red lacy thongs were sexy, but they had to go as well.

He admired her swollen fruit before sucking on her nectar. Erika's body relaxed allowing him to dig in. Familiar with her hot spots, he nibbled on her pearl until she climaxed. Xavier was far from finished. Picking her up, Xavier carried her to the hood of his truck. He placed her on it and continued to enjoy his feast.

"You are so hot baby," he growled.

"Hot for you. I need you inside of me," she pleaded.

Yielding to her pleas, he moved her back to the truck. He sat down in the back seat and pulled her on top of him.

"Ride me baby."

Erika obliged by gliding down on his erect penis. She moved slowly at first; allowing herself to adjust to the size of him. Her juices flowing like Niagara Falls, she picked up the pace, riding him like a pro. She glided him in deeper; harder. Erika couldn't hold back. She tossed her head back, letting out sounds of joy and cumming all over him.

"Oooh, I love it when you cum on me baby!" Xavier said as bright light beamed on them.

Erika leaned forward trying to hide her naked body, but it was too late. The Indianapolis Metro Police was at the door.

"You need to get dressed and step out the vehicle," said the Officer.

Erika hesitated before realizing the Officer was not going to turn around and give her privacy. She snatched up her clothes and put them on before stepping out the truck behind Xavier. All he had to do was zip up his slacks.

"Man, I thought that was you!" The Officer said. "You are the one trying to open up a club, right?"

"Ummm, yes." Erika replied embarrassed. She moved further behind Xavier to block his stares.

"Man, I saw you on the news and on *YouTube*! So you a freak for real, huh? It's cool. Look man," he said to Xavier, "you my new hero. She is fine and a freak. Look, it was some old couple who called the police, but I'm going let ya'll gone home and finish up what you were doing."

"Cool, thanks man," Xavier grinned giving the Officer a pound.

"Naw, thank you."

Erika jumped back in the truck faster than a crack head running from the police. She was beyond embarrassed. She knew the Officer was going to tell all of his buddies at the police station. She can't believe she was enjoying Xavier so much that she, or he for that matter, didn't see or hear the Officer pull up.

"What you smiling at?" Erika asked Xavier when he got back in the driver's seat.

"What I am going to finish doing to you when I get you home."

"And what makes you think we are going to finish?" she replied crossing her arms.

"Cause I know that kitty still wants me and I know that deep down that turned you on more. That fact that we got caught excited you."

"Whatever boy. Think whatever you want to," she answered. She sat back in the seat secretly smiling because Xavier was right.

Chapter 17

Xavier put it on Erika that night and barely let her out of his sight for the next few days. He wanted to be her rock, her support, her backbone. If he had too he would have given her one of his ribs. Erika's day in court was coming up and he knew she was stressed out and nervous. Regardless of how hard she tried to hide it.

"So what did your lawyer say?" Xavier asked Erika when she made it to his office. He watched as she flopped down in his oversized leather chair. She was wearing a peach colored Capri business suit and he wanted to eat her up right on top of his desk. But, now was not the time.

"That they had no case. They are just coming after me because of all the other prostitution cases. You know those 'so called massage parlors'. They are just stretching a bit too far trying to come up with something with me. Other than that she basically just went over her questions for me and how I should answer theirs," she said yawning. She wasn't necessarily tired, just worn out from being with her lawyer all day. She gazed out of Xavier's office window. She loved his view. He was on the twelfth floor, and had beautiful view of the Monon Trail. The trail stretched for over ten miles throughout Indianapolis. Hikers, bikers, runners, walkers, basically anyone used it.

"You know they are going to come at you hard right, baby?" he said coming from behind his desk over to wear she sat. Xavier pulled her out of the chair and up to him. Looking her in the eye he said, "No matter what they say, I know the real you. And nothing is going to change that."

"I know baby." She responded while putting her arms around him. She loved this man. She loved him for being there for her, for the way he made her feel, and for him not being afraid to show how he felt.

"I know we were supposed to eat lunch, but it is going on 3 o'clock. How about I finish up and meet you at your house in a couple of hours and we can go to dinner."

"That's fine. It will give me some time with Shawn. I have been so worried about going to court, that I slacked a little in the Mommy category. I mean I have been there but it was like I have been just going through the motions. Like a robot. I think I will read him a good book when I get home." She said feeling a little guilty.

"Baby, you are a great mom. Everyone needs some 'me' time every once in a while. Do what you have to do. I will see you soon." He said walking her out to the elevator.

They kissed and she got on the elevator, still looking at him as the doors slowly closed.

Leaving early enough not to hit rush hour traffic, Erika was able to make it from Keystone Crossing, back to the West side of town in less than 20 minutes. Shawn started talking a mile a minute, the moment he stepped foot in her Charger. The Preschool Academy had taken the kids on a field trip to the Children's Museum, and he was still bubbling with excitement.

"…and we saw the dinosaurs. They were big! And ooh, Mommy! Can we go to McDonalds?" Shawn said; the golden arches catching his attention.

Erika hated McDonald's. All it did for her was to make her have gas. But, today wasn't about her, so she slowed down in order to make the left turn into the entrance.

"Can I take your order?" a female voice asked with an attitude.

"Yes. May I have a kids cheeseburger meal, with ketchup and pickles only."

"Is that it?" the voice replied, now sounding annoyed.

"Yes, thank you." Erika responded politely. She did not want to give the girl any reason to spit or put something extra special in her son's food. As a teenager Erika worked in a fast food place and saw first hand how some customers got extra unwanted treats in their sandwiches. She saw everything from a manager dropping the meat on the floor and still putting it on the bun, to another male employee putting his pubic hairs on a burger. He got fired, but only after the customer complained.

There was a long pause.

"Hello?" Erika said, confused.

"You said that was it, so pull up then, dang."

Erika could tell the girl was rolling her neck and eyes at the computer. This was just another prime example of why she hated McDonald's. There wasn't any in her area so she had to go to the one on 38th and Lafayette Road. It never failed to have rudest person they could find to work the register.

Erika drove her car forward to see a female with orange and green braids in her hair; with just as colorful long, chipped fake nails, working at the window. Only three of her nails appeared to be intact. Erika never understood why some females just did not remove all the nails instead of looking crazy. If the girl had any common sense, she would have known that it was cheaper to get a full-set, instead of paying to repair all the broken ones.

Rainbow bright stuck her head out the window to collect her money and had the nerve to look Erika up and down.

"Dang, your dude let you roll in his car?" she asked, admiring Erika's Charger and the new rims she put on it.

Ignoring her dumb question, Erika handed her the $20, got her change, food, and took off.

Why is it that a woman can never make her own money and buy herself nice things?

Shawn sat in his booster seat grinning; like he had just won the million dollar jackpot. He held onto his happy meal like it was his most prized possession.

Once they made it back home, Shawn devoured his food, leaving ketchup all over his face, the kitchen table, and on the floor. Erika had him help her clean up his mess, then let Shawn beat her at a few games on the Wii. She had originally bought it because it had a lot of good educational games for him to play. She soon realized it was a great way for her to get a workout as well, especially using Wii Fit.

On my way. The text message from Xavier read. Erika and Shawn were both breathing hard from playing the last game.

Ok, I'll be ready. She sent back.

"You have fun?" She asked Shawn.

"Yes," he said in his little chipmunk voice.

"Good, now go get cleaned up. Tee-tee Shayla is about to come and get you. Shayla's son and Shawn had a standing play date. The boys would get together once a week and hang out.

"Alright!" Shawn screamed, pumping his fist in the air. "Can I spend the night too?"

"We'll see, now go and get ready." This time he took off in a sprint down the hall.

It took Xavier a little over an hour to arrive. By that time Erika had changed into a blue strapless dress, with golden designs on it and was waiting in the den for him. She kept her hair in the same style she had worn earlier in the day; flat ironed to perfection.

"You look sexy, baby," he said, giving her a kiss. "Where's little man?"

"Why thank you," she beamed. "Shayla came by and picked up Shawn for a play date to the movies with her son. He darn near wore me out playing the Wii. I thought I was going to have to drink a Red Bull or something."

"On any other day I would have said drink up because you are going to need it, but you have a big day tomorrow. I am even going to back off and not wear you out tonight."

"Please, you know that is the other way around," she joked. "So, where are we going?"

"*Fogo de Chao*, you know the Brazilian restaurant downtown," he said. Xavier already knew she had never been.

"Nice. I have wanted to go there. I heard nothing but great things about it, but that's not a place I really want to go with the girls."

"Exactly. So sit back and prepare to get romanced by your man."

Xavier smiled to himself. He wanted to take her somewhere special before her day in court. He was having nightmares himself about the sort of questions the lawyers would ask her, and the things they would accuse her of.

Not wanting to bother with finding a parking spot, he pulled up at the valet. Erika looked equally as stunning as the new Cadillac XLR-V, she had stepped out of. The valet eyes whose eyes were focused on the car when they pulled up, were now glued on Erika.

That is one lucky man. The valet thought, as he watched her enter the building.

"This place is lovely," Erika said once they were seated.

Xavier responded with a wink of acknowledgment, then, turned to the waiter who was waiting to take their drink order.

"I will have Liquor 44 and Ice Wine for the lady."

"So you do really pay attention," she said impressed. Ice was her favorite out of all wines. She and Shayla went to a wine festival last year and she had been hooked ever since.

"More than you know."

The salad bar looked amazing. Erika only put a small portion on her plate for fear of getting full too fast. She barely took two bites before flipping over her card to summon over the Gauchos, the chefs who served the meat. In an instant she had lamb chops, beef steak, chicken, pork loin coated in cheese, and the list went on. Erika was in heaven, not having to choose one particular item, but tasting all 12 items was a brilliant idea. She ate until she thought she would burst. The only other time she ate this much was at Thanksgiving.

Erika noticed Xavier was unusually quiet throughout dinner. Every once in a while she would catch him starring at her as if he had something to tell her, but never did.

"Room for desert?" their very gracious waiter inquired.

"My goodness, no," they both answered, sliding their plates away from them.

"Very well then, I will get this stuff out of your way and bring you the ticket." The waiter cleaned off their table and brought Xavier the check.

"You enjoy yourself?" Xavier asked once he paid the bill and they were waiting for the valet to return his car.

"But of course, this is just what I needed. How about you? You seem distant this evening."

"Just worried about you, baby. No big deal," he lied.

"Okay," she answered only half believing him. She figured he would tell her what was really on his mind when he was ready.

Xavier turned to a Jazz station as he drove. Erika relaxed, taking in the downtown area as they drove by. The temperature had dropped about ten degrees in the last few hours so Xavier kept his convertible top up.

When they made it back to Erika's house they put on a movie, and continued to small talk. Really, it was Erika doing all the talking. Xavier was content with her just being in his arms. Every now and then as the night went on, hc planted soft kisses on her forehead. Erika soon dozed off, breathing slowly and heavily, with her head on his chest. Xavier very soon after, joined her. They stayed this way until morning, only adjusting their position when Xavier's arm fell asleep from Erika lying on it.

Chapter 18

Dear Mama by Tupac playing on Erika's cell phone startled her out of her slumber. For a second she felt paralyzed, but quickly realized it was just Xavier's weight holding her down. Gently, she freed herself before answering the phone.

"Hello," she answered, groggily.

"I wanted to tell you good luck before you left," Mama Johnston said. Erika could feel her warmth through the phone.

"Thank you. What are you doing up so early, Ma?"

"Watching crazy Granny. You know her dementia is getting worse by the day. She is always trying to escape." Her mother owned a Hospice and Home Health Care business. One of her nurse's had quit a week earlier. Mama Johnston was covering the shifts, watching Ms. Classie, until she could hire someone else. Granny, as they called her, had severe Alzheimer's along with dementia. She had run off three nurses in less than six months. The last one quit after Granny had her arrested in the grocery store. Granny started shouting that she had been kidnapped and the nurse had a gun. The poor nurse was searched and questioned before the store owner stepped in saying that he knew the nurse and that was her patient.

Mama Johnston held the phone away from her mouth and said to Granny, "Look, I told you this is not your phone, this is my cell phone. I am talking to my daughter."

"Help! Help! I don't know this woman! She is in my house, holding me hostage!" Ms. Classie screamed in the background.

Erika couldn't help but laugh. Granny was only 86 years old and was only 4ft 8in tall, but she was a pure hellion.

"Lord help me with this woman…"her Mom prayed out loud. It took everything in her power not to hog tie Granny up, and put duct tape over her mouth. "Anyway, I love you but I have to go. Remember to keep your head up. My baby has nothing to be ashamed of."

"I love you too, Ma," Erika said, but her mother had already ended the call.

"What in the world was that?" Xavier asked overhearing Granny's screams.

"You don't want to know," Erika laughed.

"Well, I am about to go home and get dressed. I will be back to pick you up. I don't want you riding to the City County Building alone."

He left and returned in less than an hour. Erika nervously awaited him. If she did not have on acrylic nails, she probably would have chewed up her own. Grateful he chose to drive, because she was not too sure she would have made it safely. She had butterflies in her stomach and her body would not stop shaking.

Just as Xavier had anticipated, the dang media was surrounding the court house. He tried shielding her with his body the best he could. If she seemed bothered, he could not tell. Erika had her eyes hidden behind a pair of white Chanel sunglasses.

When they were safely inside the court house and past security, she told Xavier she would see him in the court room, and took off in the opposite direction to the restroom. Once inside, she stood at the sink desperately trying to pull herself together. She took controlled slow deep breaths and splashed water on her face. Giving herself a final pep talk in the mirror, she was ready.

"You ready?" Her lawyer asked when she came out.

"It's now or never," Erika replied, the last of her nervousness dissipating.

Erika walked in the courtroom with a look of determination; she held her head high and her shoulders back unfazed by the onlookers. She didn't even blink when she saw the picket signs in front of the courthouse or when it seemed like the entire city had squeezed into the courtroom. Heather was even bold enough to take a seat in the second row leaving no doubt in Erika's mind that she was the cause of all the drama. She continued down the aisle to her place at the left bench. Jade gave her an encouraging smile and Xavier grabbed her hand mouthing the words, "I love you."

A slightly overweight bailiff slowly walked in instructing the courtroom to rise for the Honorable Judge Rachel Carter. In walked Judge Carter, thc youngest judge Erika had ever seen. Not that she had seen many, but she expected an older rounder white man. This judge looked like a younger version of Judge Judy, the TV judge from hell.

Swallowing the lump trying to build up in her throat she listened as the DA tore her character apart making it seem as if she had previously worked in a whore house and was currently prostituting others out online. He had downloaded pictures from her website and even a picture she took with some other girls to promote *Passionate Playmates.* None of the items, however, included any men.

When it was time for her lawyer to speak she described Erika as a hard working, single parent, in which dancing was a way to make ends meet instead of collecting a check from the government. She described Erika's internet site as a great business move, supplying a demand to wanting customers while providing a safer environment for women, by not having physical contact with the men. She finished up claiming *Club Secrets* was a complete separate entity. It combined the love men had to have sexy woman around them, and a place to party. She even suggested that the taxes Erika would have to pay would benefit the struggling economy and put some people to work.

After hearing both sides Judge Carter adjusted her small frame in her chair before speaking to the court. "This has been a very long morning and I am sure you all can't wait to be on your way. First off I would like to say that this has been one of the more interesting cases I have seen, though I could have done without all the pictures," she said giving a glare to the DA before speaking further. "I have my own thoughts and opinions about the adult entertainment industry but those are not on trial. This issue of Ms. Johnston promoting prostitution and formerly being one herself is. The evidence does not support these claims. Ms. Johnston I do not agree with your line of work, however I do admire your cleverness and ambition. You are well onto being a millionaire before you turn 25. I say bravo for stepping into the men's only club and ruling it. I could only wish I had your business sense at such a young age. As for you Mr. District Attorney, take the pad locks and chains off of Ms. Johnston's property because she is free to open it up at her leisure."

Judge Carter slammed down her gavel letting the court know that her ruling was final and disappeared in her chambers. Keisha, Xavier, Jade, and Kenny all rushed over to her speaking at once while Heather faded into the mass of people leaving the court out of Erika's line of sight.

"I told you those bastards couldn't hold you down." Jade said.

"You looked so glamorous, walking in the door, sis. Just like mamma taught us." Keisha chimed in.

"Yes, you were very graceful," added Kenny.

"You ready to go home, baby," said Xavier pulled her into his muscular arms giving her a much needed hug.

***

Exhausted from the long day of court Erika wanted to be alone. Yes, it turned out in her favor but she was dog tired. After Xavier dropped her off she went to her room closing the door behind her. She slid off her shoes and flopped on her bed trying to free her mind.

"I know you don't want to be bothered but Kenny is on the business phone. He said your cell was going straight to voice mail and I guess you turned the ringer off the house phone. He wanted me to tell you it's very important," Tyson said barely peaking his head in her room. She was the boss but the way she was sprawled out across her bed was turning him on.

"Alright. I am up. Can you please bring me the phone?" she said sitting back up on the bed.

Thank you Jesus, he thought to himself before walking over to her. Once the phone was in her hand, Tyson hightailed it out the room, closing the door softly behind him.

"Yes, Kenny," she sighed into the phone.

"I have something of great importance. You need to know this," he said with his British accent thicker than normal.

"What is it?" She was fully awake now.

"Xavier, he ah…hard for me to say. His is the cousin of Foxy." There he said it.

"Foxy? What? How do you know?" Any person who was related to Foxy was not a friend of hers. She set up the robbery at *Passionate Playmates* and threatened Erika when she was getting locked up.

“I got a picture of him visiting her at the Women’s Prison with a note telling me to check my sources. After seeing that, I most certainly did. It seems that their mother’s are sisters and they are in fact 1st cousins.” He hated to be the one to break her heart but she needed to know.

With tears on the brink of spilling over she told Kenny thanks and that she would talk to him later. He offered to come by but she would not hear of it. She had a fish to fry as soon as she got the tears out the way. She would allow herself these tears but once they were done it was back to business.

“Xavier, we need to talk,” she said almost before he finished saying hello.

“What’s wrong baby? You sound terrible.”

“I will tell you when you get here,” she said pushing the end button on her cell.

Erika cried until she collapsed on the floor. She continued crying until it turned into anger. She felt like a complete fool, deceived, and played harder than a Nintendo WII in a room full of teenagers. She could not for the life of her see how Xavier could see her, profess his love to her, help her with her business, and lie to her for almost a full year. There should have been some signs but she came up blank trying to recall any. She wondered if this was his and

Foxy's whole plan; getting her to fall in love with him while plotting to destroy her business. She didn't doubt it if Foxy sat in her cell laughing away at Erika's expense.

Her appearance was the last thing Erika cared about when Xavier finally made it to her house. He ripped her heart out so he was going to get to see how hurt she was.

"Baby," he said walking in her bedroom, "you look awful. What's going on?"

"What's going on? How about you tell me? I know the truth. Your game is over!" She spat at him.

"Game? What are you talking about?" Xavier replied scared of the mad woman in front of him.

"Oh, so now you wanna act all innocent? I know Foxy is your cousin and you are the one who has been putting me through this hell! How could you! I love you. If this is how you do someone that loves you, you are a complete jerk. I hate you so much right now! But you know what I am done crying. I thought I wanted to hear what you had to say but what's the point? You have been lying to me all along. Now please walk out that door and the hell out of my life," she said finally taking a breath of air.

Hanging his head in shame Xavier turned around heading for the door. "I know you are mad now and don't want to listen, but when you want answers we can talk. I was going to tell you. I just couldn't seem to find the right time."

"Get out!" She screamed throwing one of her house shoes in his direction. Instead of hitting him in the head like she intended, it hit the door. Xavier sighed glancing at her one last time, then left without another word.

"Screw him," she mumbled. "I have a club to open up and there are more fish in the sea." Her words defied the pain she felt. She slumped to the floor, crying her heart out.

Chapter 19

"I can't believe I screwed it up with her," Xavier said to Foxy. They were sitting in the Women's Correctional Facility visiting room. Like clock work, he came to visit her every other week.

"I told you to be honest with Ecstasy. I never meant her or anyone else harm. I just wanted to get enough money so I could be set once I quit dancing. Those idiots, DeAndre and his boy, just lost their freaking minds shooting up the place."

"So you threatening Erika, by saying you were going to get her, was what?" Xavier never felt comfortable calling Erika by her stage name.

"I told you before I was embarrassed. Yeah I was envious of a new young girl taking my spot. But, hey, that's how the game is," Foxy answered him taking a log drag off her Virginia Slims.

"Pam your time is almost up," a slightly overweight guard said to Foxy as she walked past. She was going around the room giving everyone their 5 minute warnings.

Before leaving the table Foxy had one last thing to say to her cousin, "Look, Xavier, you love her. Go get your woman and find out who was really out to get her cause I don't think it's over yet."

"You know I love you, right?" he said kissing his cousin on the forehead as he did with every visit.

"I know," she replied, hating to see him go.

All the inmates lined up in preparation to go back to there cells. Before she was trapped again behind the metal doors she turned to Xavier.

"Now go call your woman!"

"You know the rules. No talking. Now shut up and face forward so you can go back to your cubby hole," a balding male guard with foul breath got up in her face and said.

Xavier gasped, sucking in the fresh air, when he got outside the prison walls. Being in confinement was bad enough to have to deal with the smell. The inside of the prison reeked worse than a pig farm on a hot summer day.

He had already taken his cousin's advice. Xavier had been calling leaving Erika messages for over a week and a half straight, with no reply. He left several messages bearing his heart and soul. When that didn't work he tried explaining the entire situation. They both fell on deaf ears. For all he knew Erika deleted the messages without listening to them first.

Xavier was livid with Kenny for not addressing the matter with him first. They could have talked it over man to man. He would have gladly explained the whole thing to him.

"Call Erika," he said loud and clearly so his voice recognizer would call the right person.

Beyonce singing *to the left, to the left, everything you own is in the box to the left,* blared in his ear.

"Dang she is brutal," he sighed.

Erika's caller tune changed every time he called. The last time it was Jennifer Hudson singing *Spotlight,* and the time before he heard *hit the road Jack, and don't you come back no more, no more, no more…* He had no clue who sung that one, but he knew it was meant for him. He tried calling from another phone once and all he heard was the sound of ringing. She answered that time and hung back up no sooner than he uttered a word.

After enduring his torture song he finally got her voice mail.

"This is Erika. Please do not leave a message because I will not return your call," her voice mail said in a professional tone.

Damn.

Crushed he pressed the end button, then, punched in the number for Kenny.

"Kenny speaking."

"Yeah Kenny, this is Xavier."

"Xavier? And what is it you want?"

"Listen, you were right in protecting your girl. I should have told her the truth. I never had any intentions on hurting her," Xavier rambled, scared of getting hung up on.

"But yet you did. I am not the one you need to be convincing," Kenny replied.

"I know. I have tried but she won't talk to me. I have left several messages and if I keep on it will be on the verge of stalking. The last thing I need is for the woman I love to put a restraining order on me.

"Well you did hurt her pretty bad. All I can say is keep trying. As much as I hate to mention it, she does love you. I on the other hand, believe you are nothing more than low life, rubbish, scum of the earth," Kenny said. His accent was heavier from his frustration. "If you really want to see her you should probably come to the club's grand opening on Friday."

Xavier let his negative comments slide. “Yeah I’ve been hearing about it on the radio. So she really has it all ready to go?”

“Yes, no thanks to you.”

“Look man, it wasn’t me. I was wrong yes, but all that nonsense was not my doing. You know what? I just may take you up on that offer. Do me a favor and don’t mention it to her, okay.”

“As if I would be that foolish,” Kenny huffed. Erika would have his head on a platter just for taking the man’s phone call. There was no way in the world he would tell her. He would rather swallow hot oil.

“Thanks man.”

Friday was two days away. Xavier would make sure he was there. Erika was not the one to make a scene in public; especially not in her own establishment.

Chapter 20

Devastated was not a big enough word to describe the pain in Erika's heart over Xavier. Tossing herself into her online business and preparing for the grand opening of *Club Secrets* helped with her sorrow. Not wanting to delay any longer, she planned the grand opening for two weeks after Judge Carter's ruling.

"Kenny, are you sure everything is okay? Do I need to come earlier?" Erika asked for the third time. Today was the grand opening of *Club Secrets* and she was loosing her mind. She changed her outfit five times within the past two hours. Tia, her beautician, was on the verge of burning her with the hot curlers if she didn't sit still and allow her to work her magic. She had done a favor for one of her best customers by coming to her house and was starting to regret it until she remembered that she was getting into the VIP for free.

"Yes, I have it under control. This is your night. You need to relax and arrive in style. Now let me finish making sure the bar is fully stocked," he said.

Erika was almost positive she heard glass breaking in the background before the call was disconnected. If Tia wouldn't have tightened the grip on the section of hair she was curling, Erika would have called him back. Knowing she was wearing on Tia's patience, she sat back in the chair.

"All finished!" Tia beamed at her work of art before letting Erika see the final result.

"Wow! I can barely believe this is me." Erika said taking a good look at herself in the mirror. Along with the hair, Tia did her makeup and eyelashes. Erika wanted her hair to look just like Ciara's in her *Promise* video. Even though Erika did not add weave, her hair was only a few inches short.

"Girl, I hooked you up just like those video chics. You ever thought about being one?"

"Video chic? Hell no. Video director, maybe. You know those chics don't run anything. I have to be the boss. Besides don't you remember that part in that song? *Melissa Ford drives a Honda Accord...* or something like that.

Please, I prefer my Escalade on 22's and not having to sleep with anyone to get it."

"True. Well mo hair, grow hair," Tia said blessing Erika's hair with the old superstition. "I have to go change into one of my oh so fly outfits. I still haven't made up my mind which one I am going to wear. I will see you in VIP, fashionably late of course."

Erika watched Tia sashay out her room in amusement before accessorizing her own outfit. The outfit she finally decided on was a pair of Baby Phat black high waist skinny pants with a pink off one shoulder top. She added a gold necklace with an amethyst charm that dangled right at the crease between her breasts, with matching earrings, and a Guess gold bangle watch. She stood admiring her look in the full length mirror while giving herself a pep talk.

You can do this, you deserve this, you worked hard for this, and dammit you look like you are ready to rip the runway in this outfit. Her cell phone rang interrupting her pep talk, "hello?

"You ready Chica?" Jade sang into the phone. Jade had agreed to pick up Shayla and Keisha before getting Erika so they could all ride together.

"On my way out now," Erika said giving her refection a last look before heading downstairs.

"It's your day. Take all the time you need," Jade said sarcastically taping her watch as Erika walked down the stairs. She gave Erika smooches, a fake kiss on each cheek, before they stepped outside.

"Oh my! That is sweet!" Erika said getting a look at the white stretch Hummer in front of her house.

"Surprise!" Shayla, Jade, and Keisha screamed. They were all standing up hanging out the sun roof.

"I decided to have my best friend show up is style," said Jade. She learned one thing living out in L.A., and that was image is everything. If you looked like you had money then people would flock to you in groves. If Kenny stuck to the plan then there should be a huge crowd waiting on them when they pulled up.

Erika stepped into the Hummer admiring the pink carpet, overhead lights, black leather seats, and of course the Champagne. She felt like she was truly in a video, but as the star. The Hummer was so huge it could have fit a stripper pole in it.

"Let's get this party started!" Erika said. The driver smiled at the sexy ladies and let up the tinted divider so they could enjoy themselves. He knew the perfect song to play. Soon *She Got It* by T-Pain flowed out the speakers drowning out the girls' laughter.

The ride downtown was less than ten minutes but with the heavy traffic it took almost a half an hour to pull up in front of the club. Erika looked out the window noticing the huge crowd. She could hardly believe the crowd that had formed outside the club. All eyes were on the Hummer and people were pointing trying to guess who was in it. Jade took charge telling Keisha to step out first followed by her and Shayla. Erika should be last to ensure all eyes are on her.

All of the girls were dressed to impress from head to toe when they stepped out the Stretch-Hummer. Taking a deep breath Erika stepped out of the vehicle and onto a red and black carpet matching her *Club Secrets* sign. She didn't know whose idea it was but she instantly felt like she was a movie star when the cameras started flashing. She could hear people in the crowd shouting.

"Who is that?"

"Are they models?"

"Singers?"

"That's Ecstasy! I saw her on *YouTube*. She is the owner. I don't know the other chics, but they are fine too," a young professional male informed the crowd.

"Dang, she got it like that?" commented someone.

"Ecstasy, Ecstasy!" A blond shouted over the crowd held back by a black velvet rope designed to keep the crowd at bay. "It's me Heather! What's up?"

"No she didn't?" Jade said going on the defense.

Not about to ruin her night, Erika gently looped her arm around Jade's guiding her towards the entrance. Erika doubted if Heather was there to start any drama. She probably wanted to be seen to say she knew the owner.

Bouncers opened the door immediately granting them access to the club. Erika was almost in tears as she took in her surroundings. It was one thing to see the club in the day time as it was coming together; it was another to see it at night time with the lights and her staff moving around.

Her waitresses were all in uniform with their black and pink trimmed mid length skirts and blouses that had "Can you keep a Secret?" embroidered on the back. The bartenders had on matching black slacks and button down shirts that had "Secrets" over the left breast pocket. Her bouncer's had on black as well with "Security" in white writing across the front and "the Secret keeper" written on the back. The dancers she hired were on an upper stage dressed in pink and black burlesque outfits doing a sort of rolling 20s dance to up to date music. The V.I.P. area had a red sheer curtain blocking them from the regular crowd.

Kenny walked up kissing her on the cheek giving her a thumb's up for her outfit choice. He greeted everyone else as he led them to the V.I.P. area, away from the wave of people who were finally allowed entrance once Erika had arrived. The V.I.P. area was almost full when they arrived. A few Colts, Pacer Players, and other big names had already arrived and were being entertained by some of the *Fantasy Girls* and some of the models who strictly worked the clubs private rooms.

A specific area was open in preparation for Erika's arrival. Once they were seated the rest of the people in the area held up their glasses congratulating her on the club. Erika looked out to the crowd in awe. Everyone was dressed nice and the crowd was mixed from corporate to Hip Hop. The music was bumping calling people to the dance floor with its fierce beats and sexy dancers already in place. Erika knew she had to work the crowd and meet and greet, but for now she was taking it all in.

"Look, this is your party. Let's go show them how you do it. Let's dance!" Jade said dragging Erika in the direction of the dance floor.

There was no need for Erika to protest. The bass from the music was calling out to her, hypnotizing her with every beat it made. The crowd parted allowing them room to get by.

Being the owner does have its perks I see.

Any other time it would have taken forever to fight through this size of a crowd and make it to the dance floor. The only other crowd that would even compare to this was the Black Expo.

Erika started swaying her body along with the fierce beats flowing out the speakers. The bass was so strong it vibrated throughout her entire body. Jade started dancing to her right and Keisha started dancing harder than a *So You Think You Can Dance* audition to her left. Shayla finally put down her drink and made it to the floor as a circle was forming around them. The DJ flipped the track to *Single Ladies* by Beyonce and the crowd went nuts. Everyone loved this song and was trying to do her dance. *YouTube* had hundreds of videos of it, from big fat men, to gay men, and even celebrities.

"Let's show them what we have sis," Keisha said forming a line beside Erika, who had her hand on her hip moving side to side, on step with the song. Erika moved her body to the song like she had been personally trained by the choreographer. She was working up a sweat, but it did not matter. It was her night and this was her song. It seemed as if the whole club stopped to watch them. The MC was hyping up the crowd by encouraging the girls to keep going.

"Work them hips, sexy."

"Now this is a party!"

"They won't be single for long moving their bodies like that!"

"To you other single ladies watching please take notes. This is how you get a man!"

Erika was pumped up and still on a high when the song finally ended. The crowd applauded them and begged for more. Erika waved them off saying she needed to cool down. The DJ put on another song and the crowd turned back to whatever they were doing before their dance routine.

"Dang you were working it, ma," a slightly above average guy said. He stepped in front of her to get a dance.

"Thanks."

She really wanted to go work the room but he was blocking her path. He was gyrating in front of her trying to do some of the latest dances. Giving in, she began doing a few simple moves along with him. Erika was cool with his dancing until he started grabbing her ass and rubbing his hands all over her. He made a bold move by trying to turn her around and press his crotch into her.

"Look, my feet hurt," she said pushing him off her. She needed to get the heck away from this clown. Erika hated when men tried to get their kicks off by grinding on the dance floor. Grinding was for the bedroom and not the club. If he wanted a dance like that he could go to one of the private rooms and pay one of her girls.

"It's like that? I mean I thought you liked it like that? You owning that freaky site and shit," came is intoxicated reply. He was irritated that Erika was blowing him off. He was trying to empress his friends by saying he knew Erika from high school. Now she was making him look dumb.

"Mind if I cut in?" Xavier said stepping in between them. He was sitting on one of the benches along side the dance floor and saw the whole thing. He wanted to rush the dude from behind giving him a good punch to the kidneys. He held back for Erika sake.

He was not going to ruin her evening, nor her clubs name.

"What are you doing here?"

"Yeah man, she with me," the guy added.

"This is my woman," Xavier replied. He took Erika's hand and faced the guy. Xavier's 6ft frame towered over him.

"It's cool man. My bad," he said backing off.

"Your woman? You lost those rights a few weeks ago, remember? I didn't answer your calls for a reason." Erika was smiling when she spoke but her tone reflected nothing but attitude.

Xavier disregarded her comments and pulled her in to him for a slow dance. He was right she would not cause a scene. She relaxed, moving with him to the beat of the music. His body next to hers felt so right.

Breaking the connection, Erika pulled away once the song ended.

"Baby, where are you going?"

"Not your baby. I have to work the room. This is my club and I don't want to be rude. Bye Xavier," she said releasing his hand from hers.

He watched her move towards a few people at the bar. Their eyes lit up the moment she spoke to them. She had that affect on people. Xavier did not get what he came for but it was enough for now. He knew Erika still loved him; her eyes could not hide it. Maybe with time she will come around. Xavier gave the club another once over before leaving. People were at the bar laughing and joking, the dance floor was full, her girls had taken several clients to the back for private dances, and the VIP folks were loving the full course meals the kitchen was serving. Everyone was enjoying themselves. Erika had done a wonderful job.

Keisha and Jade saw Xavier walk on the dance floor. They moved back to give them privacy, but now they wanted to know the deal. Erika finished working the room and was on her way back to the VIP area.

"I know that wasn't Xavier, was it?" Keisha asked when Erika took her seat.

"Yeap," she replied, taking a sip off her Mai Tai.

"And?" Jade said.

"And, nothing. We are done. Enough said," she answered giving them no explanation. Xavier was the last thing Erika wanted to talk about right now.

"Did you ever imagine when we were in college that you would end up with all this?" Shayla asked putting the focus back on to *Club Secrets*. "I mean look at all this. You have officially arrived and I am so happy to experience it with you."

Giving a smile as her response, Erika sat back taking another sip off her drink. She had two businesses, great friends, and lots of potential opportunities in the room. Yes, she had finally arrived and was going to sit back enjoying every moment of it.

Epilogue

"I'll teach that bitch." D'wayne said to one of his boys. "She may have gotten over and won this round but I'll be damned if her club lasts long."

D'wayne took another shot of tequila before rambling on. "Why this ho have to have everything man? Nice house, internet business, fancy rides, and now a freaking club. This is freaking bull shit."

Tony sat looking at his friend feeling pity for him. Not because he believed in his actions but because D'wayne seemed to somehow believe Erika was the cause of his life being the way it is. Tony knew Erika as well and thought she was a cool chic. She had helped him in his girl out when their mortgage rate doubled on them. He always knew she would go far when they were in college and had no idea how she ever ended up with his sorry friend in the first place.

"I mean dude, look. I had the prosecutor on her case about her club and she got over on that one. I have been online at her site for months now throwing salt up in all the chat rooms trying to get those bastards to go to other sites and they just blew me off. Hell I even had my ex girlfriend, Amber, get a job with her and she turned on me. I was hoping her sucking my Johnson on cam would cause an issue but Erika fired her faster than she hired her. I even mailed Kenny the information and pictures about Xavier and Foxy being cousins and him visiting her in jail. I don't even think that shit fazed her. She still went on and had a grand opening for the club the next week! She don't stop for nothing. Yeah man, she gonna get hers."

Hearing enough he told his boy he had to see his girl and left. "Erika better watch herself," he said walking to his car. "This fool isn't going to stop until she is destroyed."

LaVergne, TN USA
07 January 2010
169057LV00004B/13/P